For my mum, Paola.

Everyday, in every way, I'm grateful you're my mama.
Everything I am, is either from you (genetics…yay!) or because
of you.

You raised me to be confident, creative and kind, and showed me
it was okay to be different. You taught me to follow my instincts
and instilled in me the unwavering belief that I could do
anything and everything I wanted (and I really wanted to write
this book).

So, Mutti, my darling Fluffikins,
this one—the first one—is for you.

•

In loving memory of my father, Antonio, and my uncle, Barry.
Always loved. Always remembered. Always in our hearts.

Series Overview

In the Cross My Werewolf Heart trilogy, Digital Content Manager, Clarissa Hunt's life takes an unexpected turn when she awakens in a body bag after a bizarre accident claims her life. But death is just the beginning of her wild journey.

Tasked with unraveling the mystery of her newfound immortality, Clarissa finds herself thrust into a supernatural world teeming with werewolves, ancient secret societies, and perilous enemies determined to end her life, for good.

As she navigates Melbourne's paranormal underbelly, Clarissa's sense of humor becomes her most valuable asset.

Amidst the chaos, she finds herself caught between a ruggedly handsome yet abrasive stranger, and a charming and alluring doctor, both vying for her romantic attention.

A tale filled with twisty turns, mayhem and mystery, Cross My Werewolf Heart, will have you turning pages faster than xxx, and leave you breathless with anticipation.

•••

Prepare to be enthralled by this fast-paced paranormal romantic comedy set against the backdrop of Melbourne, Australia.

With a comedic flair and a contemporary tone, Cross My Werewolf Heart blends otherworldly shenanigans with laugh-out-loud moments, providing readers with a captivating and entertaining tale.

Join Clarissa on her hilarious and perilous adventure as she confronts monsters, uncovers ancient secrets, and discovers that even in the face of danger, laughter can be the ultimate weapon.

If you love reading Robyn Peterman, MaryJanice Davidson, Cynthia St. Aubin, Carrie Pulkinen and Janet Evanovich, you'll adore sinking your teeth into Esther Del Zuanne's, debut series, Cross My Werewolf Heart.

Cross My Werewolf Heart

"If I'd known I was going to die today, I'd have worn nicer underwear."
—Clarissa Hunt, Cross My Werewolf Heart

•

As if dying in a humiliating ice hockey mishap and waking up in a body bag wasn't traumatic enough, adjusting to life in a post-resurrection world is an even bigger nightmare.

Not only am I dodging a litany of paranormal beasties determined to end me for good, but my home is getting trashed more often than a Motley Crüe hotel room, my father is threatening to sue every medical practitioner in the southern hemisphere, and I'm dealing with a swath of shiny new paranormal abilities that include understanding werewolves when they, erm, speak...and smelling human emotions.

PS: yuck.

My survival—and sanity—hinge on figuring out how I came back from the dead, and why.

You'd think my situation might have improved when I stumbled across the Patrons of Order—the super-secret organization dedicated to maintaining the fragile balance between humanity and the seething supernatural realm on our doorstep.

But it didn't. In fact, my life has gone from bad to worse...and worse again.

Instead of providing answers, the Patrons only throw up more questions, confusion and lies, leaving me no closer to solving the twisty mystery surrounding my inability to die.

Of course, it hasn't all been doom and gloom. Hanging out with charismatic surgeon, Steven Nash, (have I mentioned his dazzling baby-blues? #swoon), and paranormal peacekeeper, Sonny Jones—he of the smouldering good-looks and pecs of steel—hasn't exactly been a struggle.

Now, if I could just stop all the werewolf attacks and solve the mystery of my new-found immortality, getting back to normal life would be sooooo much easier.

•

Cross My Werewolf Heart is the first book in a fast-paced, raucously funny, and wildly unpredictable trilogy featuring sassy Digital Content Manager, Clarissa Hunt, and set in the fantastical world of #fangsfurandfreaks

But, be warned, there's a juicy cliffhanger at the end and, just like potato chips, you won't be able to stop at just one!

DISCLAIMER

G'day!

Just a quick note to let you know that, despite being published in USAmerican English, this book contains lots of fun Australian content. It's written by an Australian author, featuring (mostly) Australian characters and is set in Melbourne, Australia.

There are plenty of Aussie turns of phrase, references to Australian celebrities, sporting heroes, retail stores, and places that may be unfamiliar to readers who have never lived in, or visited Australia. These are integral aspects of the story and contribute to its unique charm and fresh flavour (yep, that's flavour with a U #winkwink).

I sincerely hope you enjoy this wild trip Down Under.

ONE

IF I'D KNOWN I was going to die today, I'd have worn nicer underwear. Seriously, no one should have to draw their final breath wearing flesh-toned granny panties with busted elastic and dubious staining on the crotch.

How embarrassing.

But, don't judge, okay? It was laundry day and in my defense, it's not like I knew it was going to be *the* day.

Then again, who does?

Why was I even thinking about underwear, anyway? I was dead, for pity's sake. Well, I had been dead. Judging by the way my monitor *beep, beep, beeped* in time with my heartbeat—the EKG dancing to its jaunty rhythm—it seemed I was very much alive…again.

I pinched the bridge of my nose and tried to remember back to the previous night. Or was it the night before? No idea. Memory has never really been my strong point; it's sketchy at best. Add concussion, a heavy-duty sedative, and the remnants of what I can only assume was rigor mortis to the mix and apparently I can barely remember what was shaping up to be the worst day of my life, or my death, for that matter.

I'm sure the orderly who'd been wheeling my body from the morgue down to the basement would totally back me up, too. There he'd been, halfway through his shift, humming *Bad Moon Rising*—not very well, might I add—as he wheeled his corpse du jour (aka: me) down to the loading bay, where undertakers were waiting to transfer said corpse to their facility for "preparation" (for those of us not in the know, preparation means embalming and other gross stuff—#shudder), assuming, and quite rightly so, that the body in the bag wouldn't be sitting bolt upright on the gurney any time soon.

Of course, that's exactly what I did. I also gasped, flailed like one of those inflatable tube thingies you see in front of car dealerships, and howled for someone to LET ME OUT!

When I eventually wrestled myself out of the bag (QUESTION: why do they even have zip tags *inside* body bags? Do people come back to life often? Is it a *thing*?) I thought the poor orderly had an aneurysm or something because he was slumped in the corner of the freight elevator, eyes shut tight, chest heaving, all the color drained from his face.

When he opened his eyes and looked directly into mine, I don't know who screeched louder.

Actually, I do.

It wasn't me.

The day I died had started out much the same as any other: work, work, a couple of rowdy cocktails over lunch with the girls at Luna Bar, a spot of shopping at Highpoint, followed by a ride home in an Uber because I discovered that my car had been stolen from the shopping mall car park (that's a whooooole other story), which left me feeling less than stellar. I was going to stay home, eat my body weight in donuts and binge watch *Grey's Anatomy* (because who doesn't need an ugly cry every now and again?), but it was the AIHL season opener, Melbourne Mustangs (woo!) vs Sydney Bears at O'Brien Ice House in South Wharf, and my cousin Drew insisted I go with him... You know, to lift my spirits (and because he'd already booked me a ticket).

I should have stayed home, because if I had, I wouldn't have had to endure my rather humiliating hockey-related mishap that involved getting beaned in the side of the head by an errant puck. It wouldn't have been half as humiliating if I were, in fact, playing.

But I wasn't.

I was spectating.

I don't actually remember dying, per se; that's a little hazy, but I do remember the blinding pain when the puck slammed into my skull, and the beer and nachos I'd been carrying flying everywhere as I fell head over tail down the stairs—I'd just been on a second-period snack run when the errant slap shot by (THAT SHOULD HAVE BEEN A GOAL) ricocheted off the crossbar and over the safety glass straight into the side of my face. I toppled down the concrete stairs and landed with a sickening *crunch* at bottom.

Next thing I knew, I was in a body bag, screaming bloody murder and scaring the bejesus out of the poor orderly, who no doubt will need therapy for*EVER* after this.

Like I said: Worst. Day. Ever.

After an Academy Award-worthy dummy spit on my part, complete with biting, kicking, and a left-right-left hook combo that would put Evander Holyfield to shame, the poor nurse I'd slugged introduced me to my new best friend, Prince Valium, and I was officially in love. My extreme, albeit justified, agitation pretty quickly made way for something much more pleasant; a kind of soft, fluffy haze that was not unlike being enveloped in a cozy blankie on a chilly winter's day.

In my defense, I think I acted the way anyone who'd just risen from the dead would have. I did feel bad for punching the nurse, though. In hindsight, she didn't deserve that.

Anyhoo, that's how I found myself tucked away in a private room on the fifth floor of the Royal Melbourne Hospital—out of sight and far, far away from other patients and visitors...and the morgue, much to my relief.

The hospital was doing its darndest to keep a close eye on me and make sure I didn't relapse and die all over again. I think they were just trying to make sure they didn't get slapped with a massive malpractice claim if it turned out that they'd completely ballsed up my treatment, which looking at it objectively, they probably did.

We were at crossed purposes though, because they were hell-bent on keeping me in the damn hospital, and all I wanted to do was get the hell out.

There was a slight problem with that, though. Actually, there were several, but the most pressing was a certain lack of acceptable clothing on my part. I mean, I did have the super-stylish hospital gown they'd given me, but not before everyone in the ER had seen my goodies because, of course, I was pretty much naked when I emerged hissing and screeching from the body bag. Did I mention my crazy hair? *Urgh.*

Why were hospital gowns open at the back, anyway? Is it really that critical for medical professionals to have clear and immediate access to my butt? Was my bottom really in that much imminent danger?

And don't get me started on the weird paper undies they'd given me. I'm pretty sure they were made of coarse-grade sandpaper, fire ants, and the tears of orphans, because what else could possibly feel more uncomfortable? They were so rough, they practically vaporized my poor huhu.

I'd never missed my flesh-toned granny panties with the busted elastic and dubious staining on the crotch more than I did at that moment.

TWO

hyperosmia
/hy·per·os·mia / hī-pə-ˈräz-mē-ə
noun
: extreme acuteness of the sense of smell

THERE'D BEEN A STEADY STREAM of doctors and nurses examining me since I'd woken up. Even the registrar paid me a visit—there was an ashen-faced bureaucrat if ever I'd seen one— as had the hospital chaplain.

Apparently Reverend Thomas—not sure if that's his first name or last—had been brought in to give me last rites when I first arrived in Emergency.

Of course, the second time the Rev paid me a visit, he was much less, "Deliver our sister Clarissa, into your holy embrace, Heavenly Father," and far more, '*The power of Christ compels you!*'

I was pretty sure he wanted to douse me in holy water and send me back to the hell dimension from which I crawled. Not that I blamed him, really. I mean, I had been dead after all, and then I just…wasn't.

Come to think of it, though, of all the people I expected might have been okay with the whole rising-from-the-dead thing, it would be the reverend, because, you know, Jesus. He came back from the dead, right? Not that I was comparing myself to Jesus. Too many lepers for my taste, but we did seem to have the whole resurrection thing in common.

Was I actually comparing myself to Jesus?

I really had to go home.

I hit the red button on the remote control attached to the wall, returned it to its cradle, and started plucking at the round, sticky pads plastered to my chest—you know, the ones with the wires that connect you to all the fancy hospital equipment? In my case, the heart monitor.

Turns out, they're not as easy to remove as you'd think (though that might have had something to do with the Valium-addled buzz I was experiencing at the time), and they sting like a bitch when you rip them off.

I continued to pick and scratch at each one in turn, avoiding the one stuck close to the ropey scar that ran down the center of my chest. It's not like it hurt anymore—the scar, that is. I'd had it for ten-years and it had well and truly healed. I just didn't like it. It reminded me of things I'd rather forget.

I shook my head and ripped the second and third sticky things off like bandages (and shrieked like a banshee for my troubles). Not surprisingly, by the time I'd removed the fourth pad, the compact, but surprisingly loud heart monitor was screeching like a WWII air raid siren and dogs had started gathering outside the hospital.

As it turns out, nothing mobilizes RNs faster than a flat-lining, newly resurrected non-corpse, because in the blink of an eye, not one but two nurses all but fell through my door, and started fussing with the sensitive equipment I'd been detaching myself from. At one point I got chastised for touching the sticky pads in the first place.

The nurses, who I'll call Unibrow and Mumbles, for obvious reasons, were trying to reattach the heart monitor to my chest, when I blew out an exasperated breath and smacked their hands away.

"Stop it!" I said. "Just, stop."

Unibrow and Mumbles froze and gaped at me. "Listen, I'm sorry," I said, trying to regain my composure. For someone whacked out of their gourd on diazepam, I sure was snippy. "I'm not myself. I'm... I just... I really have to get out of here. Any chance either of you could tell me when I can go home?"

They looked at each other for a second and then back at me. "Well, that's not really up to us, Ms. Hunt," Mumbles, the younger of the two nurses, well, mumbled. "Dr. Bartholomew wants to run some more tests and—"

"Wait, who? What kind of tests?" I knew my voice sounded all high and shrill, but I really wasn't keen on being prodded and poked. Not today. Not ever. I'd had more than my fair share of that in my twenty-six years.

"I don't really know," Mumbles replied, although coming from her, it sounded more like, *I doubt there'll be snow, rmphurph...mumble... smurph.*

Hm. I knew a deflection when I heard it. Nice try.

"How about you?" I thrust my chin at Unibrow. "You got any idea what's going on?"

"As my colleague said, it's probably best that you speak with the doctor and he can advise you of—"

"I tell you what," I said, flinging back the heavy hospital covers, pulling the last of the wires from my chest with a quick, eye-watering yank, and swinging my legs over the edge of the bed. The heart monitor started screeching again, and as Nurse Mumbles stepped forward to fix it, I'm pretty sure I growled at her.

"As I was saying," I said as she retreated. "I'm going to get dressed, and then I'm calling an Uber. You have until I'm finished to find Doctor...errr..."

"Bartholomew," they chorused.

"Right. You have until then to get him here, otherwise I'll be releasing myself, okay?"

They looked at me blankly, then at each other, then back at me.

Urgh.

I don't know if it was because I was tired, or newly resurrected, but my patience was wearing so thin you could see through it. So, I waved both hands at them in a shooing motion and barked, "Scoot! Go find the doctor."

They scrambled toward the door as if I'd cracked a whip.

"Oh, and one more thing," I said, stopping them once more in their tracks. "Any chance you could hook me up with some decent clothes?"

I stood, a little wonky at first, kind of like a newborn giraffe—all gangly legs, giant head and spindly neck—and groaned. Everything hurt. And I mean that literally. My head, my body, arms, legs, even my damn hair hurt, right down to the follicles.

I stretched and tried to rub the stiffness from my limbs. It was no good. I was going to need a hot bath and major osteo adjustment for sure.

As I stretched upward and to the side, I glanced around the room. There was a wash basin in the corner, and an armchair facing a large window that framed a breathtaking view of the Melbourne skyline, a narrow chest of drawers next to the bed, and a small flat-screen TV suspended from the ceiling. There was also a door to the right that presumably lead to an en suite (I did say private room, right?) and a full-length wardrobe to the right of that. That's where Unibrow and Mumbles had stowed the clothes they'd found for me: track pants—sixteen sizes too big—and a faded Red Hot Chili Peppers t-shirt I'm pretty sure they fished straight out of a laundry hamper because there were some pretty dodgy stains on the front that may or may not have been blood.

#yuck

#beggarscantbechoosers

I wobbled to the bathroom where I pulled on the track pants and t-shirt and paused to study my reflection in the mirror.

I certainly looked the same as I usually did. I mean, I wasn't a zombie as far as I could tell; not a *Walking Dead* kind of zombie, anyway. I wasn't all gross or craving brains or anything like that. I guess I could have been a *Santa Clarita Diet* kind of zombie, maybe?

In fact, with the exception of a dark-blue bruise covering the right side of my face, and the lingering aftereffects of the rigor, you wouldn't even know I'd been dead.

Dead. Wow. Just, wow.

I splashed water on my face, gently toweled off, and exited the bathroom, all but slamming face-first into a towering man-mountain standing just outside the door. I bounced off him like a pinball and his hands shot out and wrapped around my upper arms to steady me.

"Easy there," he rasped. "We don't need you taking another tumble, now do we?"

I looked up into his narrow-set eyes framed by some seriously bushy brows. He reminded me of Santa, if Santa were a redhead.

"Dr. Bartholomew?" I said, extricating myself from his hold and moving back toward the bed. He nodded. "Great. Please tell me I can go home because I'm about done with this place."

His voice was gravelly, like a pack-a-day smoker. In fact, he smelled a little of stale nicotine and mouthwash.

"Also, before we get into that, and let me preface this with it's probably none of my business, but you really shouldn't smoke," I said, barely taking a breath, as was my way. "Because, as a health professional, you're setting a bad example, you know, for the kids. Just saying."

Dr. Bartholomew's brow furrowed, and his mouth popped open and closed a couple of times, like he was trying to use his words, but they just weren't coming out right...or at all.

He took a step back, stuffed his hands into the pockets of his white lab coat and studied me. "I had hypnotherapy three months ago," he said eventually, dropping his gaze. "Haven't had a cigarette since."

I sniffed him and screwed up my nose. "Well you might want to reconsider your laundry detergent then, because you still smell of smoke and Listerine…and a teensy bit of fear."

His eyes widened. "I beg your pardon. Did you say—"

"Fear. Yeah," I said. "What's that about?"

Funny thing was, I actually *could* smell his fear, just as if he'd doused himself in CK One. He didn't smell like aftershave, however. He smelled like sweat, ammonia, cat poop and rose water, of all things, all bundled into one icky package. It was rank, yet utterly intoxicating.

And here I'd thought the day couldn't get any weirder.

With both the Doc and I clearly confused, the extended silence was getting ridiculously awkward. I just can't do awkward silences. Or comfortable silences. Or any silences, for that matter. Silence was just wasted talk time.

"So, you're here to sign my release papers, then?" I asked.

Keeping his distance, Dr. Bartholomew removed my chart from where it hung on the wall and flipped through it.

"Let's see," he said, busying himself with the paperwork and refusing to make eye contact.

I had to suppress a giggle.

Turns out fear amuses me. Who knew?

I watched carefully as he made his way through the pages of scribbled notes, pathology reports, and EKG readouts contained in my chart.

"You've had quite the adventure, haven't you, Clarissa?" he said eventually, glancing up. "May I call you Clarissa?"

"It's my name." I shrugged.

He returned his attention to my chart.

When he hadn't spoken for another three minutes (that felt like hours), I couldn't take any more. "So, can I go home?" I asked. Again.

"Well, I don't think that's such a good idea."

"What? *Whyyyyy?*" Oh, no, that tone wasn't annoying AT ALL.

"Well, firstly, we'd really like to better understand what happened to you. I presume you would too?" he said.

Funnily enough, I didn't really care why I'd come back to life, I was just relieved that I had. As someone who'd suffered from a congenital heart defect pretty much since birth, this wasn't my first dalliance with death. And, as had been the case with all my previous experiences, I was just glad to be on the living side of the Pearly Gates.

I was about to share my near-death history with the doc when a loud kerfuffle at the nurses' station interrupted what had the potential to be a devastatingly awkward discussion.

I groaned, recognizing my father's voice echo through the otherwise quiet ward.

"I demand to see Clarissa Hunt!"

I scrunched my nose and cradled my head in my hands.

Daddy was using his, *don't you know who I am?* voice, which he generally reserved for disagreeable sales assistants (the ones who didn't kiss his ass enough), Volvo drivers (because they were all just stupid—his words, not mine) and telemarketers (because how dare they disturb his dinner and daily dose of *Home and Away*).

This was not good.

"Friend of yours?" Dr. Bartholomew asked, tilting his head in the direction of my dad's booming voice.

I was halfway through an eye roll so big I nearly toppled backward when my father burst into the room and rushed to my side.

"Clarissa, sweetheart, thank God you're alright. They told me you were dead!" I almost sagged in relief when my father swept me up in an enormous hug and squeezed the air from my lungs with an audible whoosh.

"Daddy," I squeaked. "Daddy... *air!*" He promptly released me and held me at arm's length.

"Sorry. I'm just... Well, I'm relieved. First, they told me you were dead and that I had to fly back and identify your body. Do you know how hard it was to get a flight out? It was a bloody nightmare, especially with the hurricane situation. Damned inconvenience that."

"Bahamas," I mouthed at Dr. Bartholomew who, much to my amusement, was looking both fascinated and puzzled.

"It took us nearly two days to get out."

Two days? How long had I been dead?

"Then, I'm halfway home, flying coach, mind you, what an ordeal that was, and then I get yet *another* call to tell me there'd been some kind of balls-up and you weren't dead at all! What kind of third-world *M*A*S*H* unit are you running here, mister?" Dad growled, turning on Dr. Bartholomew who, to his credit, didn't as much as flinch.

"Mr. Hunt, I'm very sorry—"

"*And so you should be.* Do you realize the trauma you've put us through? Clarissa's mother had to be sedated. *Sedated!*"

Sure, Dad. You and mum were traumatized. I'm the one who died, spent at least two days in the morgue according to your timeframe, was this close to being embalmed, woke up in a body bag, frightened an orderly to death and gave a nurse a shiner. But yeah, *you* were the ones who needed sedation.

My father, Anthony Bernard Hunt III, was a formidable man at the best of times. When he was angry, however, he could be downright terrifying. A millionaire several times over, he was the kind of person who shot first and asked questions later and right now, Dr. Bartholomew was directly in his line of fire.

"And then I find out my baby woke up in the morgue. *The morgue?*"

"Technically, I woke up in an elevator," I said, but my father ignored me. He was on a roll and nothing was going to stop his rant.

"Do you have any idea the lengths I've had to go through to keep her out of the goddamn morgue? Do you have even the slightest clue?"

Dr. Bartholomew's brows lifted slightly. "I'm sure I don't, but—"

"This hospital is going to rue the day—*rue the day*—they mistreated my little princess..."

"Ohmygod, *Daaaaad!*" I whined, mortified at his use of the pet name he'd given me when I was about six. "Little princess, really?"

He squeezed my hand apologetically. "Sorry. I know you don't like me calling you that in public."

"Or anywhere," I mumbled, and tried to figure out if I could scam some more Valium from the doc before Daddy sprung me from the hospital.

"Right. I'm sorry. I'm just—you have no idea what your mother and I have been through these last seventy-two hours."

"It's hard to imagine," I said.

"It brought back so many memories of you and Pop—"

"Daddy! Stop, okay?" I smiled. "I'm fine. Really."

"No thanks to you," he said, turning on Dr. Bartholomew again. I had to give the man credit. He certainly was one hundred percent cool under fire, unlike my father, who was all but frothing at the mouth.

"Someone is going to pay for this!" Daddy jabbed his finger at the doctor and all I wanted to do was crawl into the nearest hole and, well, die...again.

Maybe my body bag was still somewhere nearby.

Maybe I could slip back into it?

Maybe I could convince the Creedence-humming orderly to smuggle me out of the hospital? Assuming, of course, he'd recovered from his aneurysm.

"I don't care if it's you, or the hospital, or the registrar, or the orderly. I'm suing!"

I put my hand on his arm. "Daddy, go easy on the orderly," I said.

"Fine. Not the orderly. But everyone else, including the nurses, the EMTs and the chaplain!"

I felt bad for Dr. Bartholomew. He hadn't really done anything wrong. It's not like he was the one who put me in the body bag or gave me last rites. He was just trying to figure out what had happened to me.

My fingers went to my chest, and I absently stroked the ropey scar that stopped mere millimeters below the neck of the t-shirt. It was something I tended to do when I was agitated.

"Come along, princess—"

I shot my father the saltiest glare I could muster.

"Err, Clarissa. Sorry. Come, I'm taking you home. Then tomorrow, I'll take you back to the clinic—where they actually have a *clue* what they're doing!" My father stood and offered me his hand, which I gladly took.

"Clinic? Which clinic? I could send—"

Dad turned on Dr. Bartholomew and for a second, I thought he might shove him out of the way. He didn't of course. Firstly, Dr. Bartholomew was nothing short of a behemoth, and secondly, my dad didn't solve problems with his fists. He solved them the old-fashioned way. With money and lawyers and lengthy court battles.

"You don't get the chance to ask any more questions, Doc," he said. "You don't get to do anything except get your checkbook out, because I'm going to take you for every damn cent you have. You'll be hearing from my lawyer."

"No doubt," Dr. Bartholomew replied.

THREE

MY OLD BEDROOM LOOKED EXACTLY THE SAME as it had when I left home three years earlier, down to the autographed *Thor: Ragnarok* poster hanging on the back of my wardrobe door—Chris Hemsworth...yum, am I right?—and the dog-eared copy of *Twilight* on my bedside table.

When my father said he was taking me home, I presumed he meant *my* home. Instead, I ended up at my parents' house in very posh Middle Park in inner Melbourne. Ashton Court was the meticulously renovated Edwardian bungalow where I grew up. Although how anything with six bedrooms, three baths, a twenty-five-meter indoor lap pool, eight-car garage and guest cottage could be classified a bungalow, I'll never know.

Drew, had routinely told me he would have given his right nut to have grown up in our house. Wealth was not evenly distributed in our family. My parents and I were the haves; and my Aunt Bertie, Uncle Gaz, and Drew were the have nots. Per se.

Personally, I hated my parents' house. Sure, it was beautiful and elegant and full of antiques and family heirlooms, but it held a lot of painful memories for me. Painful memories, and sadness, and sickness, and loneliness, and crippling fear.

Usually the mere thought of my old room was enough to give me the heebie-jeebies. I'd sworn to myself a thousand times that I'd never set foot in it again. And yet there I was, all tucked up in my old bed, snuggled under the doona and fantasizing about leaving. Some things really don't change.

Once, there'd been another bed in the room; the bed my sister, Poppy, slept in. It's not that we *had* to share a bedroom, there were, after all, four others in the house for either of us to choose from, but as twins, we just wanted to be together, all the time.

After Poppy died—we'd both had the same heart defect, only difference was she didn't survive it—my parents dismantled her bed and put it in storage even before her funeral had taken place.

I protested, of course, but they just couldn't bear the sight of the empty bed and the daughter they couldn't save.

I drew the line at changing rooms, though. This was my room. Mine and Poppy's. We both lived there, and we would both die there, as far as I was concerned.

Of course, that never eventuated.

Lucky me.

As I lay there, contemplating calling an Uber for the second time that night, my mother bustled into the room carrying a sterling-silver tray that had once belonged to my great-great-great-aunt someone-or-other. Old. Ornate. And ugly. The tray, not the aunt.

I eyed Mum as she placed it on the dresser and proceeded to prop me up with what felt like a gazillion pillows.

"You must be starving," she said, fluffing and adjusting as I remained motionless, giving her free rein to arrange me as she saw fit. I'd learned a long time ago to just let her do her thing.

Fussing made her feel better and, quite frankly, it wasn't too shabby for me either.

"I've made you chicken soup with stars—" Because apparently, I was still twelve years old. "Fresh-squeezed orange juice and jelly for dessert."

She looked at me then and beamed. Her blue eyes were watery, like she'd been crying (no surprise there), but I could see the relief etched over her normally beautiful face. Her once-smooth skin was dehydrated, and she had uncharacteristic dark circles under her eyes. Normally, when I looked at my mother, it was like looking at her through one of those ye olde, soft-focus camera lenses. She looked all dewy, almost ethereal. Today, it looked like she'd aged twenty years overnight.

"What flavor jelly?" I asked, fighting the urge to cry as a wave of guilt washed over me. Too many times this poor woman had cared for me as I'd hovered near death. Too many times I knew she'd said her goodbyes, not knowing whether or not she'd ever speak to me again. And for the past ten years, I'd fooled myself into believing that she'd never have to go through anything like that again.

Apparently, I'd been wrong.

"Strawberry. Sorry. I know it was Poppy's favorite and not yours, but I didn't have any lime—"

"Strawberry is great," I said, covering her hand with mine and giving it a gentle squeeze. She sighed and squeezed back.

"You okay?" I asked.

"Of course," she replied. "I guess I'm a little shocked, is all. Don't get me wrong, it's not like I'm not happy to have you come visit, but to be honest, I'd have preferred a Sunday brunch over a call from the coroner."

I eyed her as a smile tugged at her lips.

"Look at you with the jokes," I said, stirring the soup and tasting a spoonful. It was hot and salty and yummy.

"Who says you can't laugh in the face of death?" she said,

trying to keep her voice light, but I knew this whole ordeal had completely freaked her out. Hell, it'd completely freaked me out.

As I slurped more of the tasty broth and star noodles (yep, twelve), I could hear my father pacing around his den as he bellowed a whole rainbow of colorful profanities at his lawyer over the phone. I could practically see Ziggy holding the handset at arm's length, for fear my father's mega-decibel ranting might perforate an eardrum if he held it any closer.

"Your father is threatening to sue every medical professional this side of the equator," she said. "I'm sure Ziggy's already picking out the new yacht he's going to buy with his retainer."

Ziggy Sheppard had been dad's lawyer for as long as I could remember. He appeased my father by filing all the [ridiculous, pointless, ludicrous = insert synonym of choice here: _____] lawsuits he dreamt up. It was practically a hobby for my father. Sometimes I wished he'd just take up golf or lawn bowls or gardening, like any other self-respecting, semiretired multimillionaire.

In return, my father kept Ziggy in tailor-made Armani suits, standing Thursday dinner bookings at the Flower Drum, and corporate box seats at the Melbourne Cricket Ground.

Me, I just thought he was a sleazebag. Ziggy, not my dad. My dad was awesome.

"Your father has also been in touch with the Myer Clinic. You have an appointment tomorrow evening," Mum said.

"Wow, that was quick," I said, still slurping more soup.

"Apparently the head cardiac surgeon was unavailable during the day, a conference or something, but you know your father, he won't take no for an answer." Mum waved her hand in the air as if to dismiss any question of doubt. "He always gets what he wants."

I smiled and nodded. Yes, he did. He's got anything money could buy, which, as it happens, was quite a lot.

"Apparently the doctor who performed your transplant is no longer there."

"Well, that's no great loss. I never liked Dr. Chaney, anyway. He was always so gruff and grumpy and really had the shittiest bedside man—"

"He died."

Oh. "Brilliant man. Truly gifted. May he rest in peace," I said, cringing. "Wait, he didn't die of heart failure, did he?"

"Let's keep our fingers crossed."

"I don't remember him that well, anyway."

"Well, you wouldn't, would you? You were such a sick girl." Mum started straightening the sheets and fussing again. We'd ventured into uncomfortable territory and she was deflecting.

"His off-sider is still there, though, the one who assisted with your transplant. Very handsome, if I remember correctly. I only met him that one time—"

"Mum, it's alright," I said, covering her hand with mine.

"Of course, it is," she said, standing quickly and taking two steps back, turning toward the door. It was clear from which parent I'd inherited my tendency to ramble when I was nervous, or agitated, or mind-numbingly sad.

"Well, I expect you want some rest, now. You must be exhausted." She wasn't wrong there. For someone who'd spent the better part of three days in eternal slumber, I was pretty pooped.

"Just leave the tray on the bedside table when you've finished. I'll come and collect it later," she said, shutting the door behind her.

FOUR

I WOKE UP SEVERAL HOURS LATER in a pool of sweat and a scream lodged tightly at the base of my throat.

Where was I? *When* was I? And what the hell had I been dreaming about? Animals. Big ones. Bears, maybe? No, they weren't really animals. They were more like monsters or something, and they were chasing me. And I was running and running. Have I mentioned how much I hate running? As far as I was concerned, there were exactly two reasons to run:

1. To catch up to the ice cream van
2. Brad Pitt.

Anyway, whatever those dream monsters were, they'd scared the bejesus out of me because my breath was coming in ragged bursts and my heart was thumping like the latest Nina Kraviz track. Not that I was a massive techno fan, to be honest. It never really made much sense to me; all *doof-doof-doof* and no substance. Now, Harry Styles—there was a man with substance, and talent, and substance and... Okay, so he was also a man with a tight tushy and the lushest hair ever, but that didn't mean he lacked substance. Right?

"Well, well, well...fancy seeing you again." A rumbly, unmistakably masculine voice cut through the darkness like a machete.

I shrieked and picked up the first thing my groping hands landed on—the book on my bedside table—and hurled it in the general direction the voice was coming. The sound of it connecting with my unwelcome guest, hopefully somewhere painful, like the face, upper chest, or testicular area, was extremely satisfying.

Shane Warne would've been proud.

There was a dull thud as the book bounced off my intruder and fell onto the shag-pile carpet.

"Hey! Watch it," he half-whispered, half-whined. "Is that any way to greet an old friend?"

Old friend? What the hell did he mean, old friend? Sure, I was vaguely aware that I *maybe* recognized the voice, but old friend? Hardly.

"I was hoping for a hug, or a handshake, at the very least."

I blinked into the darkness until the outline of a dark figure perched on the foot of my bed slowly became visible. He was rubbing his forehead where I'd beaned him with the book, and I mentally high-fived myself for my excellent, albeit entirely fluky, aim.

Shane Warne indeed.

The intruder was dressed all in leather, which I figured out because he smelled so good, like rawhide and saddle oil, but also because he made weird squeak-fart noises every time he moved.

I thought it was an odd outfit choice for a home invader, because obviously that's what this guy was. Unless there was a *ComiCon* in town I wasn't aware of? Maybe this was some cosplay gone horribly wrong?

It could happen.

I'd been to a *ComiCon* once, in Brisbane, but only because I wanted to see Jason Momoa, and absolutely not because I wanted to get my limited edition Tardis bedside lamp signed by David Tennant, who is without doubt the best Dr. Who ever. It's true. I'll fight you over it. Nope. I went for Jason Momoa. That's my story and I'm sticking to it.

Whoever this guy was, he most certainly, one hundred percent, was absolutely *not,* in any way shape or form, an old friend.

The intruder cleared his throat, regaining my full attention, and I was momentarily struck by the way his eyes shimmered an unearthly silver despite the absence of any real light in the room.

He was, well, spectacular, to be honest, with dark hair that fell in waves across his vast shoulders and giant wings that made him look ten feet tall, maybe fifteen, which, of course, was ridiculous because—wait. *What?*

Wings? Leather pants? Silver eyes? That deep, rumbly voice.

Oh. Dear. God.

My blood ran cold with the realization that I knew exactly who the cosplay man was…and it definitely wasn't an old friend.

Old hallucination, more like it.

Old nightmare, most definitely.

But, old friend? Nope.

I clenched my teeth so hard I could taste blood in my mouth. This could *not* be happening to me.

Not again.

I ducked my head under the impenetrable safety of my cozy, hypoallergenic doona (because if I couldn't see him, he couldn't see me, right?) and concentrated on not hyperventilating.

"You're not real," I said. "You're not real. You're not real. You're not real."

"Of course I'm real," he said gruffly. "You know very well I—"

I stuck my fingers in my ears, and started *la, la, la-ing*. It kind of drowned out the sound of his voice, but didn't particularly make me feel any better.

"Stop it," he said, a little less whispery this time, as he shifted from the foot of the bed and stepped toward me. "You can la-di-dah all you like, Clarissa. I'm not going anywhere."

"I can't hear you," I continued, louder this time. "Nope. Can't hear you."

I heard a muffled, "Oh for Christ's sake, stop behaving like such a child." And then the doona was summarily jerked from my body and my hands were yanked from my ears. "This crap didn't work when you were twelve and it's not going to work now."

We were practically nose to nose, his shimmery eyes locking with mine.

I squeezed my eyes shut. "My therapist warned me about this," I muttered. "I didn't believe her, but she said this could happen."

"Who, that quack, Huon? *Puh-lease*."

"She said this could happen," I continued, pretending I was all alone and talking to myself.

"She told you you'd get killed by an errant hockey puck, come back to life three days later and that your life would be in mortal danger?" he asked.

"No. Don't be daft. She told me under certain circumstances, like extreme stress, I could subconsciously revert to some of the childhood self-preservation strategies I'd created to protect myself, including but not limited to, hallucinating about, well, you," I said. "Personally, I think dying and coming back to life in a body bag qualifies as stressful, so I'm pretty sure that's what this is; a hallucination triggered by trauma. Maybe it's PTSD? Also, when you say I'm in mortal danger, what exactly do you mean?"

There was more squeak-farting as the intruder shifted his

weight from one foot to another. "If you don't open your eyes by the time I count to three, I will rip your eyelids off, and feed them to my pet unicorn. He loooooves the taste of human flesh."

My eyes sprang open and I gaped at him in horror. "You do not have a pet unicor—*wait*. No. You're just a figment of my imagination," I said with more determination than I actually felt. "I do not have to do what you tell me to."

"Seriously, you have to stop believing Dr. Huon. She's crazier than my Aunt Betty-Jean, and she thought she was the reincarnation of Joan of Arc. Which, in her defense, she actually was." He paused and pursed his lips. "But that didn't mean she wasn't certifiable."

"You know who's certifiable?" I grumbled, tugging the covers back up to my chin. "Me, that's who. Goddamn hallucinations."

"You know you were much more fun when you were a kid and you were dying, Clarissa," he said, stepping back and lacing his slender fingers together. "At least then you talked to me and didn't just act like a gigantic douche canoe."

"Hey!" I said, flashing him the saltiest scowl I could muster. "That's not very nice!"

"Neither is clocking me with a book and calling me a figment of your imagination." He bent down, picked the paperback up, glanced at the cover, and slowly raised his eyes to mine. "*Twilight*?"

I crossed my arms over my chest and huffed. "What of it?"

"*Twilight*?"

"I'll have you know; *Twilight* taps into the true teenage experience in a way that few other novels have. And...and, it brings happiness to millions of people all over the world which, if you think about it, is a beautiful thing. And so what if the hero is a sparkly creeper, which I acknowledge isn't ideal, and the heroine can come off a little insipid, but that's not the point. Besides, I'm totally Team Jacob, for the record. He's way hotter than Edward and far less…stalkerish. You know, you shouldn't judge me just because I like this book. It's rude. Plus, I've only just started reading the damn thing anyway, so you can take all your judginess—"

He eyed the dog-eared book he'd placed back on the bedside table. "Just started reading it, my ass. You know I know you're lying, right? Your mum bought you this when you were, what, ten? Eleven?? You've read it like, 10,000 times. I remember you reading it over and over when you came out of hosp—"

"This is not happening," I said. "And I'm not going through this again. You made me crazy last time, but not this time."

"You're not crazy. Well, not on this occasion, anyway." He chuckled and now it was my turn to frown at him.

"You know what, Azrael, I don't need you making fun of me or—"

"*Aha!*" he said so loudly that I startled and nearly fell out of bed. "You said my name. You do know who I am."

I ignored him, pulled the doona over my head again and rolled over so my back was to him. "Yes," I conceded. "You're the imaginary friend I made up when I was a little girl. When I was sick and lonely, and my sister had just died." I drew in a steadying breath. "And, well, I was scared I would die, too. So, sure, I believed you were really real. But I'm not that scared little kid anymore, and I know a hallucination when I see it."

He cocked his head. "Do you?"

"Yes!" I shot back.

"Could have fooled me," he mumbled.

"Yeah, well, no one asked you."

Azrael lowered himself onto the bed and lay his gigantic hand over mine, just like he used to when I was a kid.

"Clarissa," he said, his voice becoming soft, almost melodic. "I understand that seeing me again is…" he paused, "unsettling."

"There's the understatement of the decade," I huffed, pulling my hand from his.

He shot me a sideways glance. "But," he continued. "We need to talk."

"Why? I've had a very long day. I was dead and I'm pretty sure I gave a man an aneurysm. Then Dad decided he's going to sue every medical professional this side of the Westgate Bridge, and tonight I had these freaky nightmares." I scrubbed my hands down my face. "I don't know how much more I can take."

"I'm sorry. I know it's a lot. But, something's happened, and you're in danger." His voice was low and gentle. "Wait. What kind of nightmares?"

"Nightmares. You know, monsters chasing me, having my throat torn out. Regular nightmares."

"You're in danger," he said.

"Again with the danger." I was starting to think I had indeed gone completely insane and was most likely talking to a figment of my imagination.

"Yes, danger. When you died—"

"Just stop it, okay? Why don't you just go back to heaven or hell or wherever you came from and leave me alone?"

"Can't do that," Azrael said. "I've been sent to warn you."

I felt myself sag. "Sent by who? Warn me about what? And what is this danger you're being so cryptic about?"

Although if I was being honest, I really didn't want to know.

FIVE

autoresuscitation

Noun

: delayed unassisted return of spontaneous circulation after cessation of cardiopulmonary resuscitation.

"CLARISSA, I'M DOCTOR NASH, but feel free to call me Steven."

I looked up into the bluest eyes I'd ever seen, and suddenly felt a little weak in the knees, which I'm pretty sure had nothing to do with the concussion I no doubt had, and more with the snack-sized, hunk-o-burning-love standing on the other side of the desk.

Wow. Just, *wow*.

The blue eyes belonged to a man, a ridiculously beautiful man, in his late 30s-ish, dressed in dark slacks and a white Ralph Lauren polo shirt. His facial hair was too short to be a beard, but too long to be five o'clock shadow, and if it hadn't been for the stethoscope hanging around his neck, I'd have thought he was an escapee from a *GQ* photo shoot rather than a physician—a dark-haired, chisel-jawed and, if the chest discreetly hidden underneath that snug-fitting polo shirt was anything to go by, a super-buff physician who was welcome to probe my—err, you know...my, um...never mind. Let's just say he was mega-hot and leave it at that.

"Pleasure to meet you," I said. "I appreciate you seeing me on such short—"

"Actually, we've met before. I worked on your case with Professor Chaney."

"Oh," I said, a little taken aback. "Aren't you, I mean, you don't look... You're awfully young to have been a transplant surgeon ten years ago."

"Oh, I wasn't a surgeon back then. I was an intern, recruited right out of med school to practice here at the Myer Clinic. Professor Chaney was doing some groundbreaking work back then," he said. "In fact, you were quite the success story. You—"

The office door swung open and my father swept in like Scarlet O'Hara holding court at Twelve Oaks.

"Ah, Clarissa, there you are. Sorry I'm late." My father planted an affectionate kiss on the top of my head before turning to Dr. Hot Stuff and shaking his hand vigorously. "Good to see you again, Nash. Let's hope you can get to the bottom of this unsavory debacle," he said, before taking the chair next to mine.

"Daddy," I said, deliberately keeping my tone calm and even —which was in stark contrast to the cyclone of anxiety festering inside me. "What are you doing here?"

"You didn't think I'd miss this consultation, did you?"

"Well, I don't actually remember inviting you—"

"Nonsense. You don't have to invite me, princess—"

I glared at him.

"Err...yes, well. Sorry. Force of habit," he apologized. "Nash, what's the situation? What are we talking, here? Malpractice? Negligence? Gross misconduct?"

Ever have one of those moments when you were so embarrassed you just wished the ground would open up and swallow you whole? Yeah, well I was about five steps beyond that point.

Nash smiled politely at my father and turned his attention back to me. "Let's see what we have, shall we?" His fingers flew across the computer keyboard as he pulled up what I can only assume was my medical file.

"Dr. Bartholomew from the Royal Melbourne sent over your file and the report about your incident—"

"Damn straight he did," Daddy said. "I tell you, I'm going to sue the pants off him and that whole damn hospital and—"

"Why don't you let me take a look at Clarissa's file, Mr. Hunt, and we'll see what I can make of it?"

"That would be far less humiliating," I said as I sank lower in my chair. Despite being twenty-six years old, a successful small business owner in my own right, an independent woman navigating my way through life in my own unique way, and on my own terms, my father never, ever treated me like an adult. He still thought of me as that feeble kid, dying of dilated cardiomyopathy.

Urgh.

There was a long silence while Nash continued to study the pages of notes and lab reports included in my electronic file. Watching him work, waiting for my father to blurt out something mortifying as was typical, while trying not to keel over from the stress, was excruciating.

It'd been a tough couple of days.

"Well?" my father asked. "Is it malpractice or negligence? Or both? I'll get my lawyer to draw up the paperwork."

Why wasn't the ground opening up?

Nash minimized the chart on his screen, leaned back in his chair and locked me with his azure gaze. He had nice eyes. He had nice everything. Mum was right.

"Your blood work is interesting," he said, never taking his eyes off me.

"Interesting good? Or interesting I should consider a career as a sideshow freak?" I asked.

"Interesting confusing," he said, cocking his head to the side. "It didn't pick up any of your anti-virals. No immunosuppressants—"

"I'm not on any."

He frowned, opened his mouth, leaned backward and just about fell right out of his chair. Well, that sure got his attention.

"That's, well...that's impossible," he stammered. "You must be on *something*."

"But I'm not."

"But, generally speaking, transplant patients need to be on medication their entire lives. Otherwise, they... Well, they die."

I shrugged. "And yet."

"So, we sue? No immunosuppressants, that has to be some kind of negligence, right?" my father said, leaning forward in his chair with childlike eagerness. The man sure did like his lawsuits.

Nash stared at me a little longer before turning his attention to my father. "To be honest, Mr. Hunt, I can't see any evidence of malpractice or negligence," Nash said, steepling his fingers. "In fact, it looks like—"

"Are you *insane*?" my father bellowed. "They put her in a body bag!"

"Because I was dead, Daddy. Not because they were incompetent," I said.

"But you clearly weren't dead," he said, gesturing to me to help make his case. "So, someone made a big mistake."

Okay, so he had a point.

I could see Nash mulling over the situation. Obviously, someone had made a mistake, otherwise we wouldn't be sitting there. But was it a genuine mistake or had someone really dropped the ball? I could hardly wait to find out.

"How about we start at the beginning?" Nash said. "Why don't you tell me what happened?"

"I'll tell you what happened," Daddy replied. "My daughter was subject to—"

"Actually, I was talking to Clarissa, Mr. Hunt," Nash said in a voice so sweet, it was like listening to Elvis sing an Ed Sheeran ballad while swimming in a pool of molasses. "Why don't we let her tell me in her own words?"

I stared at Nash, who stared at Dad, until basically it got awkward.

"Just tell me whatever you can," Nash said, eventually breaking the silence.

"Huh? Oh, yes. Sure." I blew out a breath. "Let's see, I was dead, and now I'm not. How's that?"

Hit by a sudden wave of exhaustion, I sagged back in my seat, and sighed.

"A little more information would help considerably, Clarissa," Nash said, still as cool as a cucumber. How could someone be so calm in the face of this kind of pressure? I'd seen bigger, stronger, and more formidable men crumble under the weight of my father's interrogations. But Nash hardly seemed phased at all. He was poised, in control, and he managed to do it all while looking like a superstar.

I wonder if anyone has ever told him he looks like Chris Pine.

Nash smiled tightly and I realized that I might actually have spoken the words out loud, rather than in my head.

"I get that a lot," he replied.

Craaaaap! Definitely out loud.

"Personally, I can't see it."

"Can't see what?" Daddy asked. This was typical of him. He never really heard what other people were saying. He just barreled along with his own agenda, and then expected everyone to repeat themselves if he happened to hear a snippet of something that might interest him.

"His resemblance to Chris Pine," I replied.

"Who's he?" Daddy asked, confused. "Should we be suing him, too?"

"No, Daddy," I said, suppressing a giggle. "He's a... You know what, never mind. What were you saying, Dr. Nash?"

"You were about to tell me what happened the night of your accident."

"Right." I explained to Nash what happened, the ice hockey game, the puck, the nachos, and the body bag. I left out the part about Azrael for obvious reasons. How do you even begin to explain that your childhood bestie, who may or may not be a figment of your imagination, visited you after a ten-year absence to tell you your life was in mortal danger, without looking like a raging loon?

"So, what do you think?" I asked at the end of my tale.

Nash laced his fingers in front of him and paused. "Well, firstly, I don't think you died, not the way you think, anyway. Most likely, you experienced a phenomenon known as Lazarus Syndrome."

"What's that? What causes it?" my father asked. "Is it neglect?"

"Actually, no. It's a rare condition where a person experiences clinical death—no brain activity, no heartbeat—"

"But comes back to life after CPR has stopped being administered," I said, matter-of-factly. "Neither of which happened to me."

Nash raised his brows.

"In most instances of Lazarus Syndrome, the patient comes back within a few hours of passing away. I was dead for what, three days?"

"You certainly know an awful lot about such a rare condition, Clarissa," Nash said.

I didn't respond, just shrugged, and inhaled deeply. In my twenty-six years, I'd died three times, not including this week's debacle. And when you've died that many times before your twenty-fifth birthday, you tend to develop a bit of a fascination with strange medical phenomena, death, the afterlife, all that kind of stuff. It's not necessarily a healthy fascination, but it is what it is.

"Dr. Nash, Steven," I said, as calmly as I could. "I got hit in the head with a hockey puck, I fell down a flight of concrete stairs and I died. In fact, I was *so* dead, people were ready to embalm me. No amount of Lazarus Syndrome was going to explain that."

"Well, you might be right, but can you think of any other explanation?" Nash glanced at my father, who was conspicuously silent, and for a moment I wondered if they knew something I didn't.

"I didn't think so," Nash continued.

"In my defense, you're the doctor, not me," I said.

He nodded. "Of course. Look, I'll do more research and see if there's something else at play here, maybe there's something I missed. But for now, autoresuscitation—"

"Auto-*what*?" my father spluttered.

"That's the technical term for Lazarus Syndrome," Nash replied, and returned his attention to me. "And it does appear to be the most feasible diagnosis. Unless, you believe in magic?"

I frowned at Nash and my father shifted in his seat.

"I'm well aware there's no such thing as magic," I said, slightly annoyed. "I just don't think it was Lazarus Syndrome."

"Let me look into it and I'll be in touch. I'll call you if I find something else. Until then, I recommend some bed rest and a review in about a week. You can make an appointment with my assistant on your way out."

Nash stood and extended his hand to me.

Well, I guess our meeting was over.

"Don't worry, Clarissa. We'll get to the bottom of this."

I stood, too, and shook his hand before my father did the same.

"Could I have a minute with you, Doctor?" my father asked. "In private."

Nash nodded and I took that as my cue to leave. I didn't really want to hear about Dad's plans for suing half the medical practitioners in Melbourne, anyway.

I was just grateful I was free to go home. Home, where my shower and my fridge and my bed were. It'd been a long week and I reeked of body bag.

SIX

DAMN NIGHTMARES.

Three nights in a row I'd woken up in a pool of sweat, screaming bloody murder, and panting like an Alsatian in the Sahara.

As if coming back from the dead wasn't bad enough, now I was having scary dreams. No, not scary dreams. Night *terrors*, and they were so vivid I was convinced my feature creatures were going to leap right out of my mind and attack me in the flesh.

Tonight's installment included being chased by three towering monsters—I'm talking huge, snappy, bitey beasties with claws and fangs and red, glowing eyes—who were taking gleeful pleasure in disemboweling me and slurping up my blood and entrails…while I was still alive!

I tell you, if this was what coming back from the dead got me, then I'd take the sweaty body bag any day.

I looked at my mobile phone and checked the time: 1.45 a.m. Welp, it was as good a time as any to get up.

I snatched the bottle of Valium Dr. Bartholomew had prescribed for me when I was released from hospital, and trudged downstairs. I flicked on the kitchen light, filled a glass with water and tapped two of the small, white pills into my palm. I stared down at them, momentarily wondering if I was developing a shiny new diazepam addiction (on top of the temporary insanity I seemed to have picked up) before deciding I didn't care. I slapped the pills into my mouth and downed the water. Addiction shmadiction. I needed sleep and quite frankly, I didn't give a fat rat's ass how I got there.

Mental note, check for NA meetings in my neighborhood.

"You know, the bottle says to take one tablet at bedtime, Clarissa, not two."

At the sound of the deep, masculine voice rumbling behind me, I shrieked like a banshee and spun around, fully expecting to see Azrael and preparing to yell at him for sneaking up on me. Only, it wasn't Azrael, and I was so damn shocked, it rendered me partially paralyzed. Of course, that meant I dropped the glass on the ceramic tiles, shattering it into a million pieces, and sending razor-sharp shards skittering across the kitchen floor, effectively trapping me where I stood.

I eyed the stranger standing near my fridge and observed three things:

1. He was big. Really big. Not Hagrid big, but he was at least 6'3" or 6'4" and compared to my diminutive 5'3", he may as well have been Hagrid.
2. Secondly, *wowsers*, was this guy a looker, with long, blond hair and ridiculously striking emerald eyes that could melt the panties right off a... Well, me. Not that his handsomeness should have any bearing on the seriousness of the situation. Hot or not, he was still an intruder in my kitchen, and I was trapped on a memory foam rug. But still, yum.

3. I was extremely underdressed to be receiving company.

Most people, regular ones at least, would be screaming bloody murder at this point, trying to attract some kind of attention or help from a neighbor or passerby. Not me, though. All I could think about was my mother and how many times she'd told me to buy slippers. How many lectures had I been forced to endure, listing the 476 reasons why walking barefoot around the house would eventually kill me?

But did I listen to her? *Noooooo*. Because who *ever* listened to their parents when they rambled on about, well, anything? Nobody, that's who. And now I was stuck in my kitchen, face-to-face with yet another stranger in my home and wondering just how long my nerves would hold up under this kind of pressure.

Not long, I'd wager, even with the Valium.

I needed to stall and buy some time so I could think of a way to get myself out of yet another situation that registered 9.5 on the Richter scale of weirdness. Not that it was any tragedy having to stare at Captain Hunky Hunk (yes, that's what I'd nicknamed him. The decision had been made), but let's face it, a stranger appearing in your kitchen at 2 a.m. is never a portent of good things to come.

I raised my chin. "So, you going to tell me who you are and what the hell you're doing in my kitchen?" I asked.

The stranger's gaze swept over my body, drifting down the Guns 'N' Roses t-shirt I wore as a nightie. I was acutely aware that it didn't cover all that much, or anything at all really, so I grabbed the hem and tugged it down in a vain attempt to cover my huhu as best I could.

Fat lot of good that did. Not only was the shirt a tad on the snug side when I'd bought it, but it had shrunk beyond the point of decency after a tequila-fueled wet t-shirt situation on Hamilton Island that I'd rather not speak of.

At least I had knickers on.

"Nice shirt," Captain Hunky Hunk commented, and I couldn't help but notice the way his pupils dilated as his gaze drifted back up my body and settled on my face.

"Perv," I said.

He tilted his head before his face split into the most stunning smile I'd ever seen, and I was pretty sure my knees buckled slightly.

Good God, he was disarming.

Trapped by a sea of shattered glass, it was evident I wasn't going anywhere, not without shredding the soles of my feet, so the only chance I had of defending myself against him was to find some kind of weapon. Something within arm's reach that could inflict maximum damage in the shortest amount of time. A knife or a cleaver would have been ideal. A rolling pin would also have done the trick.

I scanned my bench tops:

- a scrunched-up paper towel
- a bag of stale Doritos
- a tub of sour cream that really should have been put back in the fridge (all leftover from the previous night's Mexican fiesta; too many margaritas tend to mess with my housekeeping skills), and
- dishwashing liquid, which I clearly hadn't used.

Unless I planned to whip up some nachos for Captain Sexy Pants (okay, so I was trying out new names for him) and lace them with spoiled dairy products and Palmolive gel, none of that was going to help me.

My back was to the sink so, without taking my eyes off him —no hardship there—as inconspicuously as I could, I reached behind and dipped my hand into yesterday's cold dishwater (PS: yuck) hoping that by some small miracle, I'd at least left a vegetable peeler or sharp chopstick in there. Because, that was likely. Chopsticks and Mexican food went hand in hand, right?

Much to my relief, my hand landed on something long and hard in the icky water. A handle!

Halle-bloody-lujah!

With what, in hindsight, was probably a little too much bravado, I pulled the utensil from the sink and brandished it in front of me like a sword.

This, of course, would have been far more intimidating if I hadn't pulled out a damned spatula and waved it around like a fly swat.

Seriously? Give. Me. A. Break.

My mysterious stranger simply smirked.

"Answer the question, buddy, who are you and what do you want?" I repeated.

'Well," he said, bending down and picking up a large shard of glass from the floor. "My name's Sonny, and I want to help you."

"Yeah, well, I don't want or need any help, Sonny, so why don't you just get the hell out of here before I kick your ass."

Sonny eyed the spatula I was gripping like it was a samurai sword. "Kick my ass, huh? Planning on flipping me over like a pancake, are you?"

I waved the spatula at him again. "I mean it, you better get out of here. I know martial arts. I could kill you with this."

Ignoring my veiled threats, because let's face it, that's exactly what they were, Sonny picked up another shard of glass and then another, cradling the pieces in the palm of his hand, his *massive* hand. Who even had hands that big? You know what they say about the size of a man's hands, right? If the rumor was to be believed, with hands that size, he must have huge...um, mittens.

"You know martial arts? Really?" Sonny said. "Let me guess, you took exactly one karate class at your local Y, what, five years ago? You thought the uniform might be cute and who doesn't love a colorful belt?" He eyed me closely, lips pursed, and brow furrowed like he was in deep thought. "You probably went there expecting to magically transform into one of *Charlie's Angels*, but instead you performed half a Kata before you had an asthma attack and quit. And if the way you're holding that spatula is anything to go by, you're probably as good a chef as you are a sensei."

My mouth dropped open and I gaped at him. Who was this guy?

"What? No. I didn't... It wasn't..." I sighed deeply and collected my thoughts. "Fine. Firstly, I went to two classes, not one, okay? And secondly." God, I hated to admit this. "It wasn't an asthma attack." I lowered my eyes. "I pulled a hammy."

He snorted and I lowered the spatula. It was one thing trying to justify my lame, short-lived karate career; it was a whole other level of humiliation trying to do it while I looked like a deranged chef.

Of course, I chose not to tell him about the five years of private Taekwondo lessons Daddy had made me take. I might not have been a punch and Kata kind of gal, but I could kick the living daylights out of most things. But that was a little tidbit I thought best to keep to myself, you know, just in case.

"Close enough." He smirked.

"So, you're what, some kind of stalker, then?" I asked and then realizing if he was a stalker, he'd probably been watching me for weeks, maybe months even. "Ohmygod, are there cameras in my house? Have you been watching me *pee*? Seriously, that's so creepy."

Sonny didn't answer, just continued picking pieces of broken glass off the floor while I mentally plotted my escape. Maybe I could still stab him in the eye with the spatula? The handle felt pretty solid.

"We're going to need a brush and pan," he said, looking up at me with those lovely green eyes. "Otherwise, you're going to end up with glass shards in your feet."

Yeah, let's face it, I wouldn't be able to bring myself to stab those pretty eyes with anything.

Despite his unannounced appearance in my kitchen, I didn't feel like this guy was a threat to me, not in a killing and maiming kind of way, at least.

He might, however, pose a giant threat to the extended period of celibacy I had going on. Not by choice, mind you. It was bloody hard to find a half-decent man, especially one who wasn't a gigantic douche, a raging mama's boy or a klepto who "borrowed" your BMW in the middle of the night, then moved to Woy Woy with a hygiene-challenged macramé artist named Persephone.

And I speak from experience.

Hence, celibacy.

I was also finding it really hard not to be distracted by my intruder's masculine energy. I wasn't sure what I found more attractive, the muscles, lots and lots of muscles, the Thor vibe he had going on, the surprisingly soothing tone of his voice, or his overwhelmingly beautiful face. Plus, he smelled a-maz-ing, like spring rain and jasmine and fruit salad.

I also wasn't sure what was more disturbing—the fact there was a stranger in my kitchen who I totally wasn't afraid of, even though he could no doubt snap me like a twig without so much as blinking, or that I was fantasizing about what he looked like under those tight, black Levi's and Bonds t-shirt.

Yummy, I'd wager.

"You're right, you know," Sonny said, rising to his feet in front of me. "I'm not a threat to you."

Erm, was I thinking out loud again? I'd already done it once today with Nash, why not again with Sonny? Or maybe he was some kind of mind reader? Because if he was, boy was I in trouble.

"And, as much as I'd like to stay and talk about what I look like under my clothes." He tapped the side of my head and grinned. *Yep. Mind reader.* "You're in danger and I'm here to—"

"Let me guess, you're here to save me because something wicked this way comes and only you can protect me? Like I'm *sooooo* pathetic and *sooooo* utterly useless that I couldn't possibly take care of myself? How's that? Am I close?"

"Eerily, with the exception of that last—"

"Well, listen up, mister. I'm not a child anymore, okay? I don't need to be coddled or protected. Why does everyone think I'm some kind of a hopeless wussy? Okay, so I died, but I'm back aren't I? I... I..."

Sonny pursed his lips and frowned.

"What?" I said, dropping the spatula back in the sink and crossing my arms over my chest.

"I'm thinking nerve-strike," he said, taking a step back. "Daddy issues, maybe?"

"Oh, shut up," I grumbled.

"Listen, I'm sure you're perfectly capable of taking care of yourself under normal circumstances. But your circumstances are about to get extremely abnormal."

"Yeah, yeah, I know. Azrael gave me the spiel already," I sighed, shaking my head. "Supernatural danger. Monsters breaking down my door. Like I said, I've heard it all."

Sonny stiffened. "Wait, you know Azrael?"

I blinked at him. "Well, sure. Do *you* know Azrael?"

"By reputation only."

"He has a reputation? Really?" I asked. "Whatever you do, never tell him that. It's the kind of shit that'd go straight to that gigantic head of his."

The inherent weirdness of the situation wasn't lost on me. Up until three days ago, I'd been convinced that Azrael had been a figment of my childhood imagination. Then he reappears after a decade and not only does it turn out he was very much real, but that he's also some kind of paranormal rock star.

"How do you even know Azrael?" Sonny asked. "He's not exactly a people person."

"To be honest, I haven't as much as thought about him for ten years. But then I died and came back to life and he just appeared at the end of my bed two nights ago and—"

"He's been *here*?" Sonny asked.

"Well, no. He was at my mum's, but—"

Before I could finish my sentence or find out how in the hell Sonny even knew about Azrael, an almighty crash shattered my otherwise silent house and gave me such a shock I'm pretty sure I peed a little.

Again, so glad I'd put undies on.

I screeched and leaped behind Sonny—shattered glass be damned—and flinched as the tiny shards dug into the soles of my feet.

Well, that was going to require some antiseptic.

Peeking around his massive frame, I watched as three of the biggest—what in the hell were they even? Bears? Yetis?—burst into my living room, snapping and snarling, upturning furniture, and tossing aside everything in their path as they lumbered toward us.

Did I mention my living room was on the second floor of my town house? Second. Floor. Which meant whatever they were, they had to have jumped at least four meters, from a standing start, to get up there. Talk about a seriously impressive vertical leap.

Sonny took a deep breath and squared his shoulders. "Damn, they're here," he muttered.

"Who's here?" I squeaked.

"It's not so much a who, more of a what," he replied, pulling a sword out of what looked like a quiver on his back and swishing it around in front of him.

Who even was this guy, sexy Robin Hood? Because I could totally get into that.

"Okay then, *what* are they?" I corrected.

"Werewolves," he said.

I snorted. Ah, yes, werewolves. Naturally. What else would they be? All big and drooly and tearing up my house.

I gaped up at Sonny who looked to be scoping the situation.

"Are you crazy? Werewolves aren't real!" I said, still cowering behind him.

"You wanna tell these guys that?" he said, motioning at the hulking beasts eying us from the threshold of the dining room. "Because I'm sure they'd get a kick out of being called figments of your imagination."

"This can't be happening. Seriously," I said, rubbing my hands through my hair. "This is just one of my crazy dreams. That must be it. I'm still asleep and this is like in the movies, when the hero thinks they've woken up, only they haven't really, and then freakier, scarier shit happens just as their guard is down and—*ouch*! *Hey*!"

I rubbed the spot on my arm Sonny pinched and scowled at him. "Son-of-a... What the hell was that for?"

"You said you thought you were dreaming, so I pinched you. It hurt. Ipso facto, you're awake," he said, deadpan.

"Ipso facto?"

"It's Latin. It means—"

"*I know what it means*," I said, with a massive eye roll. "You know, I'm beginning not to like you very much." I rubbed the sore spot where a lovely bruise was already forming.

"I really don't care if you like me or not," he said.

Well, that was just rude.

"What I do care about is not being carved up like last Sunday's roast chicken by these guys. So, if you don't mind, I have some werewolves to deal with. Also, just so you know, referring to yourself as the *hero* of this story..." He used air quotes when he said hero and shook his head. "Not cool."

"I'm not trying to be cool, you jackass."

"Well, you're succeeding." He grinned at me.

I glanced back at the werewolves (it's weird even saying that, not to mention realizing they were actually real) who, if I didn't know better, looked like they were amused by our bickering.

"Are you really sure they're werewolves?" I asked, still not willing to accept what was clearly in front of me. I mean, coming back from the dead was one thing, having my nightmares become reality another, but werewolves being real? Nope. Just, no. "Maybe this is just some kind of freaky flash mob? Or drop bears? They could be drop bears."

Right on cue, the largest of the giant creatures pounced from my living room straight onto my kitchen counter (easily 10 to 12 meters), landing on all fours and sending cooking utensils and the remnants of last night's dinner flying in all directions. Then, it threw back its head and howled so loudly, everything in my house, including me, shook.

Sonny gave me a sly, side-eye glance. "Yeah, probably not drop bears."

Smart ass.

The beast was massive, maybe two meters tall, covered in matted ginger fur. Its snapping jaws were filled with crooked, razor-sharp canines at least twenty centimeters long, and its eyes were black as coal. It stank of dampness and stale sweat and general yuck and I could feel the bile rising from my gut as I inhaled the acrid stench.

"God, that's gross," I said, clapping my hand over my mouth and nose. "When's the last time that thing had a bath?"

"Let's not insult the lycan, Clarissa, okay?" Sonny said.

I rolled my eyes. "It's just going to make mincemeat out of us anyway," I said. "I doubt my snide remarks are going to make things—"

"Quiet!" the werewolf roared and both Sonny and I staggered back a few steps. "Your bickering is giving me a headache!"

I froze and gripped Sonny's shoulders.

"Um, is this like a T-Rex situation?" I asked. Sonny had firmed up his position between me and the werewolf and was still swinging the sword back and forth to keep the beast at bay.

"What?" he barked

"You know, like in *Jurassic Park*. If you move, the T-Rex can see you. If you don't, it can't. Is it the same with this…this thing?"

Sonny shook his head. "This *thing* could see you if you were three miles away, hiding in a lead-lined box in an underground cave. Makes no difference if you move or not."

Well, looks like playing possum just wasn't going to cut it.

"You," the werewolf growled in a gruff voice that seemed to rattle and reverberate through my entire body. It was the single most terrifying thing I'd ever heard and I'd been to a Slayer concert. "Step aside. We have no quarrel with you."

I sagged a little in relief. Thank God. Whatever it wanted, it wasn't me. It wanted Sonny.

Phew!

"We're here for the woman."

Bugger.

"Me? Why the bloody hell are they here for me?" I asked.

Sonny just glared at me and cocked his brow. "Who?"

"What?"

"Not what, who. Who's here for you?"

"The werewolf." I motioned toward the hulking beast that, if I didn't know better, had a puzzled look on its face. "Why is it here for me?"

"You can understand me?" the werewolf said, leaning in and sniffing the air. "How is that possible?"

"How is any of this possible?" I muttered.

Sonny turned and looked at me, brows raised. "Something you'd like to tell me?"

"Like what?"

"Like why you can understand lycan?"

"I have no idea! Up until five minutes ago, I didn't even know werewolves existed. Now you're telling me it's a skill to understand when they talk?"

"Vocalize. They don't talk. They vocalize."

"What-everrrrrr!" I was really losing my shit.

"What's it saying?" Sonny asked, oblivious, or indifferent, to my inner turmoil. Clearly this was just another day at the office for him. Whatever his office was.

"It's saying it has no quarrel with you. It only wants me," I said, hoping he had a plan to get us out of this predicament.

Sonny looked from the werewolf to me and back again. "Unfortunately, a quarrel with Clarissa is a quarrel with me," he said. "So, I guess we're at an impasse."

Whoever this guy was, I didn't care. All I knew was he was willing to fight werewolves for me, so as far as I was concerned, he was okay. Even if he was a jackass. A sexy, yummy jackass.

"Step aside, Peacekeeper," the red-furred beast growled and I'm pretty sure I whimpered.

"What's a Peacekeeper?" I asked.

Sonny's eyebrows shot up. "What?"

"A Peacekeeper. What is it?"

"Never mind about that," he snapped. "Just stay behind me." He squared his shoulders and focused on the werewolf on my bench. "I'm sorry, but you cannot have her," Sonny said. "If you want her, you'll have to go through me first."

"Good idea," I said, nudging Sonny forward. "Take him. He'd make a much tastier snack than me."

"Snack? Seriously?" Sonny said, never taking his eyes from the werewolf. The other two snarling beasts stood sentry behind it, snapping and growling, but keeping their distance.

"You said they had to go through you." I shrugged. "I was just facilitating."

"This is your last warning," Stinky Wolf snarled. "Step aside or we will kill you both, slowly."

"Fine," Sonny said, stepping aside and exposing me to the werewolf. "Be my guest."

"Hey!" I said. "What happened to, 'You need to go through me, to get to her blah, blah, blah?' What was that? Lies? And since when do you understand werewolf-er-ish, too?" I asked.

"You just offered me up as a snack. What did you think I was going to do, fight to the death for you?"

"Well, yeah. Kind of."

"Sorry, pet. I take my job seriously, but no one's worth getting shredded by that," he said, pointing at the werewolf.

"Job? What job? Has this got something to do with being a Peacekeeper? Because I don't even know what that is but it doesn't sound like—"

"Enough!" the werewolf howled as its paw darted out, quick as lightning, and batted Sonny aside like a cat swatting away one of those little plastic balls with the bells inside.

Sonny sailed across the room, three feet in the air, before slamming into my china cabinet and shattering its entire contents. How in the hell was I going to explain all this to my insurance company? I'm pretty sure rampaging werewolf wasn't covered in my home contents policy.

I scrambled to Sonny's side and ran my hands over his body. No wounds as far as I could tell, but my word, the pecs on this man! Rock hard and impressively large.

"Fondling a defenseless man. Not cool, Clarissa," Sonny said without opening his eyes.

"I'm not fondling, I'm… Are you even injured?"

"I've felt better," he said, sitting up. His eyes locked on something behind me and widened. "Shit."

I felt the werewolf's breath on my neck before I even heard it.

I stood, turning slowly only to find the ginger beast looming over me, drool hanging from its mouth, claws making a high-pitched screeching sound as they raked across my Italian marble floors.

It inched closer and, with slow, deliberate movements, it sniffed me, which, between you and me, was more than a little disgusting.

"You're not afraid of me," it said, a touch of surprise in its gravelly voice. "You're confused, but not afraid."

I blinked up at the beast. "How do you even know that?"

"My lycan senses are much more sophisticated than lowly human ones," it scoffed. "Your hormones are like the evening news. Thanks to your primitive genetic make-up, I see, hear and smell everything."

"Can you smell yourself over there, buddy? Because wow, you've got some BO issues going on."

The werewolf snorted. "You'd be wise to shut your mouth, woman."

"Or what? Because, so far this week I've died and come back to life, been visited by my childhood imaginary friend who, it turns out, not so imaginary, and is some kind of celebrity in your creepy-ghoulie world. My father is threatening to sue every medical professional in the Southern Hemisphere, not one, but two strangers have invaded my personal space and now, thanks to you and your mind-numbingly gross sidekicks, my apartment is trashed. I mean, you couldn't just knock? You had to charge in here and tear everything up and what, now you're going to kill me?"

"You talk too much," the werewolf said.

"So I've been told."

"You won't be talking too much shortly, though."

"And why's that?"

"Because you'll be dead."

"Been there, done that. It didn't stick."

"It will this time. When I kill you," the werewolf snorted, "you're going to stay dead. I'm going to tear you apart and pick your flesh from my teeth with your bones. After that, your apartment and everything you own will be mine to plunder as I please...including the Peacemaker."

"Actually, he's not mine. We only just met—"

"Shut up, or I'll shut you up myself."

I bristled and lifted my chin in defiance. "We'll see."

"Indeed, we will," it said, crouching. The movement made the hairs on the back of my neck prickle and I got an uneasy feeling in the pit of my stomach.

This was so not good.

"In fact, why don't we see right now?"

Without a moment's hesitation, the enormous werewolf lunged at me, and at the same time, its two off-siders charged at Sonny, pinning him to the floor with their full body weight. It was clear killing me was something the ginger, buck-toothed, smelly werewolf wanted all for itself.

With surprising agility, I sidestepped the beast, avoiding the full force of its massive paw as it came down hard on my shoulder and knocked me to the floor.

I rolled to the right and scurried under my dining table, just as it bought its other paw down, missing me but obliterating one of my dining chairs.

"A swing and a miss for the mongrel," I said, before realizing Sonny was right and it probably wasn't such a good idea to taunt the werewolf.

Stinky Wolf roared so loud, even the sentries flinched, and before I had any time to regroup, it grabbed the table I was cowering under and flipped it over, leaving me fully exposed.

"Prepare to die," the werewolf growled as it descended on me.

You know how they say your life flashes before your eyes when you're about to die? Well, it doesn't. Your mouth just goes dry and *My Way* plays over and over in your head.

Weird.

From the corner of my eye, I spotted Sonny's sword, just within arm's reach, and quick as you like, I reached out and grabbed the hilt. I was so relieved to feel the heavy weight of the weapon in my hand, I practically whooped with delight. Instead, I clutched it tightly and just as the beast launched itself at me again, I raised the sword, thrust upward and plunged it deep into its chest. The werewolf reared back, the sword still protruding from its rib cage, and howled bloody murder. It staggered back, falling against the remains of my dining table chairs and tumbled to the floor.

"Holy shit!" I said, scurrying backward. "I did it! I. Did. It! I killed the werewolf! Did you see that, Sonny? Did you see?" I looked to where Sonny was still struggling against the sentries. He'd managed to get to his feet but still unable to get free.

"Clarissa!" he yelled. "Behind you!" Sonny's voice seemed so far away; it was like he was at the end of a long, long tunnel.

I'd been so busy congratulating myself for my speed and bravery, I hadn't actually realized that the ginger werewolf wasn't dead at all. Instead it had risen to its feet and was standing in my obliterated kitchen with Sonny's sword protruding from its chest.

And from what I could tell, it was really pissed off.

Slowly, it pulled the sword out, licked its own blood off the blade and opened its massive jaws in a maniacal grin. "I'm going to take great pleasure in ripping your throat out," it growled, and I knew there and then that I was in serious trouble.

Defenseless, I clambered backward, trying to put some space, any space, between me and the werewolf. But I knew I had nowhere to go, and there was nothing I could do.

This was it.

The end.

Again.

The last thing I remember was turning toward the sound of Sonny's voice, his desperate screams echoing in my ears as the ginger werewolf crouched on all fours, jaws wide open, and lunged at me.

SEVEN

THREE DAYS.

That's how long it took me to come back from the dead the second time.

Three days, and my body had completely healed, my vital organs kicked back into gear, and I woke up to a bright and shiny new world where werewolves were real, I was seemingly immortal, and a very attractive Peacekeeper was cooking pancakes and bacon in my kitchen.

I'd been awake for about an hour before I mustered the energy to haul myself out of bed and face the carnage the werewolf attack had caused to my apartment.

Werewolf attack.

If I hadn't seen it with my own two eyes, I wouldn't believe me either. I mean, it was simply too ridiculous for words.

Werewolves were not only very much real and roaming the streets of Melbourne, but they were also bursting into houses at 2 a.m., killing unsuspecting people in their kitchens and causing decorative devastation the likes of which hasn't been seen since season one of *Selling Houses Australia*.

It was all about as bizarre as my new propensity for dying and not staying dead, and finding out my Guardian Angel wasn't actually a figment of my imagination, but rather a real, live man. Or non-man.

What were angels, anyway?

Of course, I knew there had to be a logical explanation for everything that had happened. I was just hoping it wasn't insanity. With any luck, with the right amount of caffeine, I'd be ready to figure all this weirdness out and have this whole mystery sorted by lunchtime.

I looked at my watch: 10:48 a.m.

Okay, maybe I'd have it sorted by dinnertime.

I swung the bedroom door open and padded down the stairs, fully expecting to have to weave my way through the remnants of my lounge suite, splintered floorboards and so much shattered IKEA. Instead, I was immediately struck by how little debris there was. In fact, as far as ground-zero destruction zones go, my front room was decidedly…intact. There wasn't as much as a dust bunny floating around, which given my cleaning skills, was a miracle unto itself.

Everything was pristine; I mean, it was display-home pristine. No. It was *Three Birds* pristine. Everything was styled within an inch of its life, and I had absolutely no idea how it had gotten that way.

But I did have an idea who might.

Sonny was seated at my dining table—my brand spanking new, not at all smashed into a million tiny pieces, dining table— and looked every bit as delicious as I had remembered him.

For a moment, when I'd first woken up, I thought I'd imagined the whole thing, and that Sonny was merely a figment of my overactive, under-sexed imagination. But when I eventually started moving and stretching my muscles back to life, the familiar aches and stiffness from the rigor let me know that I hadn't imagined any of it.

The smell of freshly cooked bacon was punctuated by the scent of fresh-brewed coffee, strawberries, and industrial-grade disinfectant. The combination was so pungent and overwhelming I thought I might actually puke. I didn't, thankfully, but it was all I could do to stop myself from barfing all over my Uggs. It didn't help that there was also an incessant buzzing sound that, if it kept up much longer, was going to drive me up the fricken wall.

I paused in the doorway of my kitchen and watched Sonny eat his breakfast with a delicateness I would have thought would only have been reserved for royalty. He was a massive man, broad and muscular. Shouldn't he have been tearing into a wild boar's leg and swilling mead? Instead, he was gracefully chewing French toast with his pinkie raised elegantly, and flicking through... I squinted at the cover of the magazine he had propped up in front of him. *Better Homes and Gardens*?

"It's rude to stare, you know," he said, without looking up from whatever DIY article had captured his attention.

"And it's rude to break into someone's house unannounced in the middle of the night, but you don't see me getting all nit-picky about it." My voice was raspy, like a pack-a-day smoker, and a hot pain shot down my throat with each word I spoke.

Sonny looked up at me, smiled and yep, my knees went a little weak, again. Damn, that man.

Before I could even attempt to say anything else, he stood, walked to the sink, took a glass from the dish rack and filled it with water.

"Drink," he said, passing it to me like it was the most natural thing in the world; like he absolutely belonged in my kitchen, in my home, in my life.

I blinked up at him. This was so far from natural or normal, I couldn't even *see* natural and normal from where I was.

"Go ahead," he said, gesturing to the glass. "You'll feel better."

I hadn't realized I was thirsty until the cool water hit my palette and soothed the back of my burning throat. I downed the water in three large gulps and then did the same with the second glass after Sonny refilled it for me.

"Thank you," I said, eventually, a little breathless (which may or may not have something to do with Sonny. I couldn't be sure) and croaky.

"It's good to see you're finally awake," he said like someone who'd clearly been waiting for me to get my butt out of bed.

"How long have I been, you know," I asked, motioning to the ceiling in the general direction where my bedroom would be.

"You mean dead? Three days."

"Three days? Three *daaaays*! How could I have been dead for three days?"

"That's how long it took you to come back this time."

"My God," I said, the tangled knot of anxiety coiling deep in my belly. "How am I going to explain this to my parents? They must be freaking out by now!" I snatched my phone off the kitchen bench and tapped in the PIN.

"Don't worry. I took care of them."

I stalled and gawked at Sonny. "Took care of them? How did you 'take care of them?'" Coil. Coil. Coil. "Ohmygod! You didn't kill them, did you?"

"What? No, of course not. What kind of person do you think I am?"

"I don't think you're a person at all," I said, returning my attention to the phone and opening the text message app. "I have no idea what you are."

When I tapped Mama in the Messages app, I noticed the inordinate number of texts that apparently "I'd" sent her over the past three days.

I eyed Sonny. "You did this?"

He smiled, and my panties started melting yet again.

"Thank you," I said.

"I'd reserve your thanks until after you read the messages, if I were you." He grinned.

"Why? What did you say?" I asked, but he didn't reply, just kept grinning like a big, sexy idiot.

"Relax. I just told her you decided to go away for a few days and that you'd call them when you got home."

"Oh," I sighed, relief washing over me.

"Then I sent her photos of food and of some woman's feet in front of a pool, and the problem was sorted." A broad grin split his face and he folded his hands across his chest.

"Thank you," I said.

"I may also have mentioned that you'd gotten lucky with the cabana boy and the two of you scored some pretty good weed."

"You did *not*," I shrieked.

"Oh, but I did. His name is Carlos and you're both pretty high right now."

My brows shot up. "I swear, Sonny, I'm going to throttle you." I thumbed through the texts I'd supposedly sent my dear mummy, and sure as hell, there they were, text after text going into great detail about the awesome marijuana we'd been smoking and all the amazing... Amazing... Ohmygod, all the amazing sex we'd been having.

I was going to kill Sonny.

"Hey, don't look so freaked out. Your mum seemed pretty happy for you. Check for yourself." He pointed at my phone. "She said she was glad you were having such a great time and to keep sending photos of the buffet."

I was about to check and see exactly what catastrophe Sonny had created, when I noticed the red circle in the top right corner of my Instagram app. In it, the number 987.

"Shiiiiiit!"

"What?" Sonny said. "I told you, she's okay with—"

"No, not my mum, you dufus—although we are going to talk about that. No, I mean this." I pointed at the Insta app.

Sonny peered at the phone, back at me, and shrugged. "What?"

"Um, are you blind? Look at how many notifications I have."

"That's what you're worried about?" he asked.

"Yes! These are for work."

"You work?"

"Of course I work."

"What do you do?"

"I'm a Digital Content Manager."

"A what?"

"A Digital Content—you know what? Never mind." I kept trying to clear my throat but the raspy, croakiness just wouldn't budge.

"You might want to go easy, there," Sonny said, pointing to my neck. "You experienced a massive throat trauma. You probably shouldn't speak much for a few days, maybe even a week—"

With a loud, and I have to admit, less than ladylike cough that sounded like I was hacking up a fur ball, I cleared my throat and grinned at Sonny. "Thanks, but I think I got it," I said, smooth as you like.

"Or not," he said. "How? How is that even possible?"

I shrugged. "See, one thing you probably don't know about me, is that it's practically impossible for me to stay quiet for more than a few minutes. Nothing can stop me from talking, you know?"

Sonny looked a little startled. He was cute when he was startled. Hell, he was cute all the time.

"I'm beginning to see you're quite the talker—and fast healer, too." He took the glass back to the sink and rinsed it before putting it on the dish rack.

I nodded. "Seems so," I replied, lifting my hand to my neck

to check the massive throat injury he'd mentioned. Bracing myself for pain and oozing wounds, I grazed my fingertips gently across my throat. I could feel the skin beneath was tender and swollen.

"How do you feel?" Sonny asked.

"I'd feel better if I knew what the hell happened to me," I replied. "I mean, I didn't dream the whole werewolf thing, did I? They really did bust up my place and attack us... Or was it all a hallucination?"

"Well," he said, sitting back down and sliding the chair opposite him out with his boot-clad foot. He motioned for me to sit, which I did, despite wanting to tell him off for putting his feet on my furniture. "It definitely wasn't a hallucination; you were attacked by a werewolf right here," he said, tapping the table top. "Beverley ripped your throat out and you bled out there." Sonny pointed to a spotless section of the kitchen floor, indicating where I'd allegedly perished at the hand of the house-destroying werewolf.

"Who's Beverley?" I asked.

"The werewolf."

My eyes widened and I gaped at him. His name is *Beverley*?"

"No, *her* name is Beverley.

"That was a *girl*?"

Sonny nodded.

Wow.

"And then she threw you through these glass doors." He pointed at the pristine glass sliding doors that lead out to my balcony. "And then you were just a stain on the driveway."

Charming.

I blinked and thought back to the night of the attack. I remembered waking up from a nightmare (which, PS, was remarkably similar to what transpired in my kitchen). I remembered getting a drink and shattering the glass when Sonny startled me. I also remembered the three giant werewolves breaking into my house, two of them pinning Sonny down while the big, orange one beat the stuffing out of me. But I definitely didn't remember having my throat ripped out, or being flung through a glass door. Surely I'd remember details like that, wouldn't I?

"How did you get away from the werewolves?" I asked, smelling a rat.

No, literally. I could smell rat, although how I knew what a rat smelled like, I'll never know.

Mental note: buy Ratsak.

"I didn't have to get away. Once they'd done what they came to do, they released me."

I narrowed my eyes at him. "You're telling me they simply let you go? Just like that?"

He nodded.

"Why would they do that?"

"I'm a Peacekeeper. Being responsible for my untimely death would be..." He paused, pursing those plump lips of his. "Let's say it'd have dire consequences for the perpetrator."

"And my untimely death? No one gives a shit about that?"

"Apparently not. Although, your death doesn't appear to be as permanent as they might have expected."

I reached for my neck again. It was still sore to the touch, but it was almost like I could feel it healing beneath my fingertips; the cells regenerating; my skin knitting itself together.

Surely if my throat had been ripped out by a werewolf (I still can't believe I'm even entertaining that notion) it'd be, well, ripped out still. I wouldn't be healing. I'd be dead.

I came to the conclusion that Sonny was either talking bollocks and that there was more to this than he was telling me, or the hockey puck had in fact killed me, and I was currently in hell. Part of me was hoping it was the latter.

"I don't believe you," I said, standing up and planting my hands on my hips. "Where's the blood? If I'd had my throat ripped out, there'd be blood spatter everywhere. But it's spotless." I paused. "And why isn't all my stuff destroyed? I mean, those werewolves ripped through this place like a cyclone. How is this..." I spread my arms wide to take in the whole kitchen and dining area. "Even possible?"

Sonny picked up his coffee cup, took a swig and smiled. Did I mention he had swoon-worthy dimples? I mean, eat your heart out, Mario Lopez, swoon-worthy.

They made it hard for me to focus.

"The clean-up crew came through two days ago," he said. "They fixed everything."

I ran my hand over the perfectly smooth surface of the dining table that I remember had been obliterated in the werewolf fracas, and frowned.

"Clean-up crew?"

"Yes, as in, a crew that comes in to clean things up. The name is pretty self-explanatory."

God I was really beginning to hate him.

"Yes, but how is this even possible?" I repeated.

"I told you, clean-up crew."

"Yes, yes, I heard you the first time, but this is, I mean, how is it humanly possible for anyone to clean up that train wreck in just a couple of days?" I asked.

"Who said anything about humans?" He eyed me over the brim of his cup, and winked.

"Who are you even, and what else about this insane situation don't I know?"

"So many things," Sonny said, motioning to the empty chair again. "If you'd sit, maybe I could explain a few to you."

"I don't really want to sit," I said.

"But you probably should. You received some bad injuries. You need to take it easy."

I pointed to my neck.

"Or not," Sonny said, squinting at what I could feel was completely healed skin.

"I'm not injured. I'm not feeling tired. I just want you to tell me what the hell is going on."

He sighed, clearly wrestling with some internal conflict I wasn't privy to, nor did I really care about.

"Okay, then. So, you were definitely attacked by a werewolf," he said

"Yeah, I got that part. I was attacked and you're like, who, Van Helsing? Fighting the werewolves and saving innocents from eternal damnation?"

Sonny snorted. "Van Helsing hunts vampires. I said werewolf."

"Fine. So who hunts werewolves, then?"

"Me," he replied.

I nodded. "Well, if you don't mind me saying so, you suck at your job."

His brows shot up. "Oh?"

"Well, I got attacked, didn't I? My apartment got totaled, and according to you, I died a pretty gruesome death. Does that sound to you like something that should have happened if *somebody* was doing his job properly?"

Sonny chuckled and then a huge smile spread across his face.

"I mean, how many other people have you failed to save from certain death? How many people have woken up one morning thinking it was just another day, instead they get mauled by Bella Lugosi—"

"Lon Chaney."

"*Whatever*! Who else have you gotten mangled like a chew toy before they died?"

Sonny was silent for a long while. A disturbingly long while. Perhaps I'd said something wrong? Perhaps I'd hurt his feelings?

"You're the only one," he said, sheepishly.

"I'm the only one, what?"

"The only one I wasn't able to save, *and* as far as I know, you're the only person who's survived a werewolf attack."

My mouth popped open. "What, like, ever?"

"Ever."

"Wow." A million questions jammed their way into my mind the same way peak-hour commuters sardined themselves into the 5:08 express train to Watergardens on a Friday, but "Why me?" was the only one that managed to wiggle its way out and find its way to my mouth.

He scrubbed his hands over his face. "If I knew the answer to that, I'd…"

"Wait!" I screeched, startling not only Sonny, but also Miss Miranda, who had been sunning herself on the other balcony just off the dining room. For a moment, she looked like she might jump-jet straight over the railing, but she managed to right herself before she took the three-story drop.

Miss Miranda, my six-year-old, green-eyed, long-haired black cat was a birthday gift from my parents. She was stocky, chatty, very demanding when it came to mooching pats off *anyone*, and to be honest, I was never sure if she really liked me, or she really liked the fact that I fed her, watered her, brushed her, and cleaned up her poop.

"Does this mean I'm going to turn into a werewolf?" I asked.

"What? Why on earth would you think that?

"Why wouldn't I? I've watched *An American Werewolf in London*. I know what happens," I said, feeling the agitation rising in my gut again. "You get attacked by a werewolf on the moors, or in my case, the dining room. You survive, and then on the next full moon, you turn into a werewolf, kill a bunch of people and get shot in an alley. Is that what's going to happen to *me*?"

"Do you always believe everything you see in the movies?" Sonny asked.

"Kind of." I shrugged.

"Well, you shouldn't."

"Oh, excuse me, but it's not like I have any other frame of

reference, is it? They don't exactly teach Werewolf 101 at Melbourne Uni."

"Still, *An American Werewolf in London*, not a documentary, Clarissa."

"I… But…" I sighed. "Fair enough. So, you're saying I won't turn into a werewolf at the next full moon?"

Sonny tilted his head and shrugged. "Um, I don't think so?"

"You don't think so? You don't *think so*?"

"Actually, I don't know."

"What do you mean, you don't know?"

"I told you, no one's ever survived a werewolf attack before. So, I have no idea what's going to happen to you next full moon."

"Well, there must be someone who does know, right? Surely?"

"As a matter of fact, there is," Sonny said. "And, as it happens, he's requested the pleasure of your company."

"Has he? Who is he? What does he do?"

"Let's just say he's my boss, and he—"

"Where is he? Is he far?"

"No. He's pretty close—"

"Cool, what are we waiting for?" I hitched my thumb at the door. "Let's get a wriggle on, shall we?"

Sonny stood. Good golly, he was tall. "Actually," he said, looking at his wristwatch. "He's expecting us a bit later, and I've got a few things I need to take care of this afternoon."

I opened my mouth to respond, to tell him to screw his errands; that it was far more important to find out if I was going to wolf out at the next full moon or not. But when I saw Sonny's lips thin and his jaw tighten, I thought better of it and decided to shut up instead.

"I'll be about a couple of hours," he said, striding into the kitchen and depositing his coffee mug in the sink. "That should give you enough time."

"Enough time for what?" I asked, confused.

He looked me up and down with a somewhat pained look. "Enough time to, you know." He waggled his finger at me. "Fix yourself up."

"What do you mean, fix myself up?"

"Hair, makeup, clean clothes. You look..."

"What's wrong with the way I look?"

"Nothing, if you were a street urchin."

Jackass.

I looked down at myself, then absently ran my hand through my hair. It felt like a bird's nest...made of steel wool...after a cyclone. Oh, boy.

"Fine," I conceded, trying unsuccessfully to pull out some of the knots. "I'll freshen up."

"Good idea," he replied.

"What should I wear?"

"I don't know, something nice. Something less...you know. This."

I decided to ignore the last jibe and focus on the fact that I had the chance to frock up. "Okay, well, I have the Stella McCartney I bought for my cousin's engagement, or maybe the Sass & Bide. I've been dying to wear that and it would look fabulous with my strappy—"

"I don't need a running inventory of the contents of your wardrobe, Clarissa," he said. "I just need you to go do whatever it is that you do to make yourself presentable."

"Hey!"

"I'll be back later to collect you."

"Fine," I huffed, pointing at the door. "Feel free to leave whenever you like."

Sonny tapped his wristwatch. "Time's a ticking."

"Yes, Sir. No problem, Sir."

He leaned in close to me and I was overwhelmed by the smell of ripe, plump peaches. What a heady aroma. It reminded me of the cheap cask wine my friends and I used to drink when we were in high school. In hindsight, it was truly awful stuff. It was so sweet, I'm surprised all my teeth didn't fall out just at the mere memory of it. But, boy did it smell great.

"I like it when you call me sir," he whispered.

A hot flush swept from the top of my head down to the tips of my toes. "I'll be sure to remember that."

"Please do," he said with a wink before striding toward the front door.

Holy guacamole, he was tempting! He was also a douche. *Go and make myself presentable.*

Who even says that?

I'll show him presentable.

I'll show him just how presentable I can be.

Sonny paused at the door, hand on the knob and looked back at me. "You might want to have a shower while you're at it," he said, scrunching up his nose. "You smell like you died."

EIGHT

WHEN SONNY SAID HE WAS TAKING ME TO MEET HIS BOSS, I guess I'd imagined we'd be going to a chic little bistro somewhere in the city. You know, one of those trendy places with yummy tapas, salsa music streaming from a state-of-the-art sound system, and bottomless pitchers of margaritas. (I really like Mexican food. I think every occasion is better with tacos and tequila.) Hence the four-inch stilettos and Sass & Bide cocktail frock I'd bought for my friend, Jessie's, Hen's Night last April. Of course, that wedding never actually went ahead on account of Jessie finding out her fiancé, also named Jesse, had been schtupping his personal trainer, Bevan, which wouldn't have been half as bad if girl-Jessie hadn't been schtupping Bevan, too.

I ended up wearing the Sass & Bide to Melbourne Cup instead and won second place in Fashions on the Field for my troubles. That netted me a nifty magnum of Champagne (the real stuff, not the faux bubbles you get at BWS), a bouquet of flowers the size of a goat, a pamper voucher from Endota day spa… Oh, and a check for a cool $5,000.

Not too shabby for Clarissa.

What I hadn't expected, however, was to be trudging through the dimly lit streets of North Melbourne, trying to not make eye contact with the weirdos trolling around the area (who in their right mind wears a tutu, jelly sandals, and a mankini in the middle of winter?) and developing what would later become the blister to end all blisters on the heel of my left foot.

When Sonny came to a sudden stop outside an unassuming building on Lonsdale Street, I almost slammed straight into the back of him, pulling up just in time to prevent making a perfect impression of my freshly make-upped face on the back of this jacket.

"Why are we stopping?" I asked, smoothing down my skirt.

"We're here," he replied, pointing at the building.

I looked up at the simple façade, read the sign hung on the exterior fence and frowned: St. Francis' RC Church.

"We're where?"

"Here," he said.

"We're going to church?" I asked, acutely aware that my designer frock was probably a tad too short and a smidge too booby for Friday-night mass.

"No. We're going *into* the church. There's no mass this evening."

"Oh, bloody hell," I grumbled, pulling my skirt down and wrapping my pashmina snugly around my shoulders. "You could have told me."

"And miss out on seeing you in this outfit? I don't think so," he replied, his sweeping gaze down my body made me quiver from the inside out. "I must say, you fill out that dress in all the right places and in all the right ways." He smiled.

I felt my cheeks heat and thanked my lucky stars that it was too dark for him to tell I was blushing.

"Thank you," I said, looking at my shoes. God, they were pretty, with their satin-ribbon detailing and diamanté straps. "But I can't go in there dressed like this. It's not appropriate."

"Well, it's too late to get prudish on me," he said.

"You don't understand, I need to go home and change into something less..."

"Scandalous?"

"Hey! This isn't scandalous. I'll have you know this is a lovely dress."

"Then there's nothing to worry about then, is there?"

I crossed my arms. "I'm not worried. I'm just saying that this dress isn't appropriate for *church* and I'm not going in there until you take me home so I can change."

He smiled and shook his head. "Sorry, pet. There isn't any time. We're late as it is."

"Well, I guess we're at an impasse, then."

"Are we?"

"We sure are. Unless you're planning to carry me in there, I'm not budging."

"Oh my God, put me down!" I screeched, as I struggled to pull my skirt down, and my neckline up, all while hanging upside down as Sonny carried me into the church over his shoulder.

Unless you're planning to carry me in there.

Famous last words.

Had I known picking me up was going to be so effortless for Sonny, I might have reconsidered my ultimatum. I mean, I'm not overly hefty, but I'm certainly curvy enough to give the average man pause before he tried to sling me over his shoulder like a sack of potatoes and carry me twenty meters without so much as breaking a sweat. Of course, I was coming to realize Sonny was far from average, and if I was completely honest, I wasn't sure he was even a man.

I had totally underestimated the situation.

Once we were inside the narthex, Sonny had the decency to put me down and grinned as I readjust myself so that all my bits were tucked back into my dress. Sort of.

"You're despicable, you know that, right?" I said.

"Just one of my many endearing qualities," he replied, dimples flashing.

I tried to ignore them.

"Yeah, well try something like that again and I'll punch you right in one of your other qualities and we'll see how much you like that."

Sonny laughed and gave me the once-over. "I look forward to it. Now, shall we?"

I merely stared at him, unmoving.

"Am I going to have to carry you again?" he asked.

"I'd like to see you try."

"You know if you just did as you were told, we wouldn't need to keep having these discussions."

"Like that's ever going to happen."

"Fine." Sonny stepped toward me and I stepped back. "Don't worry. I'm not going to pick you up again."

Instead he reached out and took me by the elbow as he guided me into the church toward the altar. I wrenched my arm from his grip and placed my hands firmly on my hips.

"How about you just stop with the bullsh—"

"Ah, ah, ahhh…" Sonny said, pointing up. "You're in the house of God now. You should probably ease up on the swears."

I pursed my lips and frowned at him. I had lots of swears whirling around in my head at that moment, but I was willing to save them until we weren't in God's house. You know, just in case he was actually home.

"Then how about you explain exactly what we're doing here, and I might come along nicely? Also, why haven't you burst into flames yet? I would have thought someone of your moral caliber would be a big pile of ashes by now."

"I'm going to ignore that," he said, a massive grin splitting his face. Damn it, why did he have to have those adorable mega-dimples?

"And I told you, we're here because it's time for you to meet the boss."

"The boss of what?"

He chuckled. "Everything."

"What? You mean..." I pointed to the altar.

"Who? Father Nolan?" he asked.

I motioned toward the altar again. "No, dumb-dumb. You know...*God*," I whispered.

Sonny laughed and shook his head. "Don't be ridiculous. As if He'd waste his time on the likes of you."

I felt a rush of annoyance flame my face. What was so wrong with me? Apart from the swears and the repetitive dying, of course? And my addiction to designer dresses and *Geordie Shore*. And my Thursday night tequila and nacho ritual. And my... Never mind. I didn't care what Sonny McHottie thought of me, anyway.

"Who then?" I asked.

"If you stop talking and come with me, you just might be able to find out for yourself." Sonny turned on his heel and headed directly for the altar with long, purposeful strides. I couldn't help but notice the way his jeans hugged his pert butt and muscular legs. He was toned and tight in all the right places and my nether bits tingled enthusiastically in response.

"Coming?" His voice boomed through the otherwise empty church and startled me.

"Nearly. What? No. What?"

"Are you coming or not?" He pointed behind the altar as if I was meant to know what was back there and tapped his boot-clad foot. "Someone's waiting to meet you."

NINE

"ARE WE THERE YET?" I whined as I groped my way down
the poorly lit stairwell. "We've been walking for hours!"

"We've been walking for exactly..." Sonny paused to check
his wristwatch and shook his head. "Eight minutes. Just how
unfit are you? I mean, we're walking *down* the stairs. You better
not complain this much when we're walking back up."

I opened and closed my mouth, but nothing came out. How
can someone so hot be such a pain in the butt?

"And yes," he said. "We're nearly there."

Of course, he was lying.

Sonny had opened a trap door behind the altar and lowered
me about six feet into a tiny, torch-lit room. It was damp and
became one hundred times more claustrophobic when he slid his
massive frame down next to me and grabbed one of the flaming
torches from the wall.

Being that close to Sonny was intoxicating, exhilarating and
utterly terrifying—an unsettling combination. He was all muscle
and smooth, tanned skin, with his perfectly defined pecs and his

ridiculously chiseled abs, which I'd had the pleasure of feeling when I felt him up… I mean, patted him down, and checked him for injuries, FFS, in my kitchen.

And the way he smelled! It was like fruit salad and testosterone. Yum.

"This way," Sonny said, heading down the first few steps. "Follow me."

I saluted and trailed along behind him as we descended farther and farther beneath the church.

When we eventually got to the bottom of the stairs after what felt like F-O-R-E-V-E-R, we came face-to-face with the biggest, heaviest looking door I'd ever seen. Easily three meters tall and a couple wide, it was held in place by huge iron hinges and adorned with an impressive, intricately engraved knob.

"Wow." I nearly wept in frustration. "Looks like you're screwed now. I mean, I know you think you're a tough guy and all, but I don't see how you're going to break this down."

Sonny reached into the front pocket of his jeans and pulled out a beautiful gold key, which he slid into the lock under the ornate knob and turned with ease. He winked as the lock clicked and the door swung open. "Sometimes, we need to use our brains, Clarissa, not just our brawn." He smiled, and my knees buckled just the tiniest bit.

"Whatever." I stepped past him, careful not to make direct contact because, you know, #internalcombustion, and my mouth popped open. There, right under St. Francis Church in North Melbourne, was another Cathedral complete with rectory, marble altar and stained-glass windows that stretched up at least ten meters to a vaulted ceiling.

Wowsers.

"Where are we?"

"Level two," Sonny said.

"This is amazing. I never knew—wait, level two? How many levels are there?"

"How many do you think?"

"I think I have no idea."

"You never read Dante?"

I pffted. "Of course, I've read Dante. What kind of an igno-ramus do you think I am?"

I hadn't read Dante.

"Apologies, but I wasn't sure you'd been able to squeeze *Inferno* in between all those *Twilight* books." Sonny's grin rivaled the Cheshire cat's.

"How did you... When were you in my room?"

"Someone had to check on you, you know, while you were regenerating. I can't help it if you keep a clearly well-loved copy of *Breaking Dawn* next to your bed."

Smug bastard.

"Didn't he write about hell?" I asked, desperate to change the subject and vaguely remembering something from my third-year English Lit class at uni.

"Who, Dante?"

"No, Stephanie Myers. Of course, Dante!"

"Amongst other things." Sonny smiled.

"So, you're taking me to hell?"

"You'll just have to wait and see."

By the time we reached level nine, the same number of levels in Dante's *Inferno*, I may as well have been in hell. I was sweaty, and hungry, my feet were a mangled wreck, the shellac from last Monday's mani-pedi was chipped to the schizen and everything hurt.

I was not a happy camper.

The lower we'd gone, the hotter it had gotten. Hotter and smellier and yuckier.

The beautiful stained glass and marble features of the cathedral made way for damp walls and slimy floors.

My feet were throbbing. I still had my heels on, because despite Sonny's suggestion, I wasn't about to take them off and walk through this cesspool barefoot. I mean, blisters were one thing; slime and fungus between my toes, noooooo thank you.

The final great door on level nine opened into a beautiful foyer lined in exquisite mahogany panels. Gone was the slime and ooze dripping off the walls; replaced with wood and gilt frames, stretched canvases, frescos—masterpieces from every artistic period you could ever imagine. Impressionism. Cubism. Renaissance. Expressionism. Surrealism. You name it. They had it.

Some of them I recognized: Degas, Van Gogh, Michelangelo, Matisse and Dali. Others, not so much.

When I squinted at the signature on the very first painting, I recognized it immediately: P. Cezanne.

Hmmm.

And then the second painting: Claude Monet.

Okaaay.

And the third: Jackson Pollock.

Had we walked all the way to The Louvre? It was possible. It felt like we'd been walking for days and—

"Stop gawking. You look like you've never seen a painting before," Sonny said, hustling me away from the impressive art collection and toward what looked like, of all things, a reception desk. It had a high, redwood counter, creating just enough of a barrier between visitors and the stiff-looking woman sitting behind it.

"Are they, you know, originals?" I asked, nodding at the giant Andy Warhol-esque screen print hung behind the reception desk. It depicted a stunning, dark-haired man with impossibly high cheekbones and pools of onyx for eyes, replicated on four panels in hot pink, yellow, purple, and red ink, reminiscent of the series Warhol had completed of Marilyn Monroe, Elizabeth Taylor, and Mick Jagger.

"Of course," Sonny said. "Does this look like the type of place where they'd hang knockoffs in the foyer?"

"No, this looks like the type of place Dracula would summer," I replied.

Sonny glanced down at me through ridiculously thick lashes and tutted. "The Count prefers Ireland in the summer. It's better suited to his delicate constitution."

I gaped at him, but before I could ask any of the five billion Dracula questions that had instantly popped into my head, the prim woman behind the desk, who wore a beige, button-up blouse and a hair bun so tight, it pulled her eyebrows way up into the center of her forehead (PS: not a good look), peered over her horn-rimmed glasses and cleared her throat. She was attractive enough, in a plain kind of way—like popcorn, only without the butter. And I guess the bad hair and crusty-scalp situation was nothing a bottle of Head & Shoulders couldn't fix.

"Mr. Jones, lovely to see you again," she said, her cheeks turning a delicate shade of pink as she took in Sonny's impressive form.

"The pleasure, Rebecca, is all mine."

Rebecca giggled, and her cheeks darkened to a stunning crimson.

"Oh, puh-lease," I said, rolling my eyes.

Rebecca pursed her lips and scowled at me. Looks like I wasn't going to be making any friends down here.

"And who might you be?" she asked, eying me warily.

Before I could say a word, Sonny grabbed my hand and yanked me hard to his side. "This is Clarissa Hunt. Vincent is expecting us."

"He is?" I asked.

"Yes."

"Awesome." I grinned. "Who's Vincent?"

Rebecca gasped as if I'd asked who Elvis was. I couldn't even think of any famous Vincents, except Vincent Price.

Were we waiting to see Vincent Price?

Wasn't Vincent Price dead?

Vincent Van Gogh? No. Also dead.

"Please take a seat and I'll let him know you're here," Rebecca said, gesturing to the waiting area opposite the reception desk.

We sat on an overstuffed settee that was far prettier than it was comfortable, with all its scratchy fabric and ridiculously stiff back. It was like sitting on those old-school church pews with the fold-down kneeling thing that was guaranteed to bruise your patella and make your legs go numb in less than a minute, only less pleasant.

I leaned into Sonny. "So, seriously, who's Vincent?"

"I told you, he's the boss."

Oh, FFS. It was obvious I wasn't going to get any answers from this guy. I'd just have to wait until I met this mysterious Vincent and find out who he was for myself. With any luck, he'd be a bit more forthcoming with the facts than mien bodyguard over here.

I let my eyes roam around the enormous hall, up to the vaulted ceiling that was adorned with richly colored frescos of pearlescent clouds, willowy vines, and pudgy, ruddy-faced cherubs.

"We commissioned those from Da Vinci in the early 16th century and had them shipped here in the mid-1800s," Sonny said as he watched me ogle the exquisite panels.

"Da Vinci? As in *Leonardo* Da Vinci?" I asked.

"No, Darrell Da Vinci. He's a plasterer from Craigieburn."

"Oh, right. I… wait, *who*?"

"Of course, Leonardo Da Vinci."

I narrowed my eyes and prepared to fire off a tirade of colorful words but thought better of it. We were still in God's house. Well, under it. We were in God's basement and I still had to mind the swears.

We sat in silence for a few minutes before curiosity got the better of me.

"So, what's the story with you and Miss Stuffy-Knickers over there?" I whispered, motioning to Rebecca. "Are you two an item?"

Sonny turned his head and shot me a dazzling, panty-melting grin. "Why? You jealous?"

"Hardly," I scoffed and hoped I sounded convincing.

"Then why do you care?"

"Just curious," I said in the lightest tone I could muster.

"Would you be angry at me if I told you that Rebecca and I were an item?"

"I've been angry at you since the moment we met," I said. "So, probably yes."

"And what if I said there was nothing between us?" He leaned in close, his lips brushing the shell of my ear with the barest of flutters, sending a jolt of white-hot electricity from the base of my neck straight down between my, well, let's just say it was an area that hadn't seen much action in the last six months.

I'm sorry, did I say months?

I meant *years*.

"How would that make you feel?"

Hot! Horny! So damn needy, I could just weep.

"Nothing. I told you, what you do and who you do it to… with, makes no difference to me," I lied.

"Alrighty then."

When the double doors that led to the mysterious Vincent's office clicked open, I was relieved for the distraction.

"He will see you, now," Rebecca said, smiling at Sonny before narrowing her catlike eyes at me.

"Thank you," Sonny cooed, shooting her a confident wink that made her flush again.

Either that woman had a terrible case of idiopathic craniofacial erythema (it's a thing—Google it) or Rebecca seriously had the hots for Sonny. And I mean, *baaaad*. I felt a tight little knot form in the pit of my tummy. Did they actually have a thing going on? He'd never really answered my question. Evasion is generally a sign that someone is lying, right? I wondered what kind of relationship they had. Was it serious? Recent? Had they, you know...done it? I mean, she was attractive, blushing and sweating aside, and he certainly came across as a big enough man-whore to want to deflower this Victorian floozy. So, I guess there was a good chance that it was a big fat yes. They'd seen each other naked.

I don't know why the mere thought of Sonny and Jane Eyre doing the humpy-sweat made me want to lunge at her, drag her down to the toilets by her bun and drown her in one of the stalls, but it did. I didn't, of course. Maybe I was overtired. Maybe I was doing my usual and reading more into things that weren't actually there (a nifty little trait I'd inherited from my father). What else could explain why I felt so...so...jealous? Was Sonny right? Was I possessed by the green-eyed monster?

"Come on," Sonny said as he stood, shaking me from my disturbing internal diatribe. "It's show time." He led me by the elbow to the double doors, pushing them open with his free hand. "Just try not to say anything stupid, okay?"

"Bite me," I replied.

"With pleasure."

TEN

THE OFFICE BEYOND THE DOUBLE DOORS was every bit as opulent as the reception area. Every square inch of wall space was adorned with photographs of the stunning man I'd recognized from the Warhol prints behind the reception desk, with every celebrity, monarch, politician, and religious leader imaginable. Gandhi, Bill Gates, Queen Elizabeth II, Joe Biden, a couple of popes, all The Beatles, Beyoncé, the Dalai Lama, Quentin Tarantino, Oprah Winfrey, and Mr. Urban, both Keith and Karl.

Who *was* this guy?

The room was lit by flaming torches, similar to the one Sonny had used to guide us down the fifty gajillion stairs to get there.

Directly in front of us were two armchairs that matched the settee we'd sat on in reception—overstuffed and under-comfortable. I was going to need an osteo treatment after today's torturous activities, that's for sure.

Mental note: call Dr. Jade and book an appointment with her

for tomorrow. Yes, I said tomorrow. Dr. Jade may be the most highly sought-after osteopath and Harvard-educated clinical business strategist in the country, but I could always count on her to fit me in for a treatment.

I wasn't her number-two VIP cardholder for nothing. (And no, I don't know who number one was, but I confess I do secretly hope one day they move interstate, so I can get bumped up to top spot.)

Beyond the chairs was a desk at least two meters wide, featuring beautifully hand-turned legs and topped with a twenty-centimeter-thick slab of Carrara marble.

Cha-ching! Someone around here was flush.

Behind the desk was a throne, not that I'd ever seen a throne. It looked like what I imagined a throne would look like, with its high back and gilt carvings, brass studs, and rich emerald fabric.

Seated on said throne was a man so ethereally elegant, he literally took my breath away. Not in the same way that Sonny took my breath away, with his bulging biceps and fine, fine ass. No, throne guy, with his lean physique, refined bone structure and graceful manner, was as beautiful as the paintings that hung on the gallery walls.

He looked up, affording me a much better view of his alabaster skin, high cheekbones, and eyes so dark you couldn't tell the iris from the pupil. His square jaw was flecked with dark stubble that matched his raven hair.

This guy didn't belong buried in this crypt in the bowels of the city. He belonged on *Vampire Diaries* or *Grey's Anatomy*; you know, shows that starred all the pretty people. Or a catwalk in Paris, at the very least.

"Close your mouth," Sonny snipped. "You're drooling."

"Hardy, har har." I knew he was being a smart Alec, but on the off-chance he wasn't, I wiped the corners of my mouth with the back of my hand.

Ha! Minimal drool.

Mr. Elegant looked oddly familiar, and that's when I twigged this was the guy from the Warhol prints and celebrity photos.

Again, who *was* he?

Had he known Warhol?

No, he couldn't possibly have. This guy was thirty-five years old, tops. Warhol died in what, '86, '87? That would mean Mr. Elegant had to have been, like, seven years old when the prints were made. So, that had to mean the Warhol was fake? And if the Warhol was fake, the rest of the art was probably fake, too. Including the Da Vinci panels. Right?

They probably *were* done by Darrell Da Vinci from Craigieburn after all.

How stupid did they think I was?

"What is wrong with you?" Sonny asked. "You look like you're about to pass out from thinking so hard."

I opened my mouth to give him what-for but was interrupted by Mr. Elegant. "She's trying to work some things out, aren't you, Clarissa?"

I looked up to see him twirling an exquisite Montblanc fountain pen between his slender fingers.

Was everyone around here a mind reader?

"Sonny, it's good to see you again," Mr. Elegant said, replacing the cap on his pen and rising from his throne. He glided—or was it glud? Was glud even a word?—around the gigantic desk and stood directly in front of us. "And you brought me a present."

His eyes flicked to mine, and he gave me a quick once-over. The faintest of smiles quirked the corner of his mouth.

Was that good?

Or was he sizing me up for something?

Why did I suddenly feel like I was in one of those lobster tanks you see at Madame Wong's or, Death Row for Crustaceans, as I preferred to call it, waiting for someone to pick me out, throw me into a pot of boiling water and smother me in garlic butter.

Was I on the dinner menu?

I balled up both hands into tight fists, ready to take a swing if either of them made a move toward me. I was little but I would go down fighting.

Much to my relief, Mr. Elegant lifted his hand, and offered it to Sonny, who took it and, to my astonishment, pressed his lips to its back while taking a deep bow.

"Vincent, it's a pleasure as always," Sonny said, rising to his full height again. "May I introduce Miss—"

"Clarissa Hunt," Vincent said, offering me his hand, too. "Yes. I've heard much about you."

I stared at his proffered hand, then at Sonny and back at Vincent.

What the hell did he expect me to do? Was I supposed to kiss it? Because, yuck. How poncy and pretentious could someone be? Who even kissed hands anymore?

Vincent cleared his throat and nodded at his hand. I was clearly taking too long to do something—*anything*—with it, which only made me more uncomfortable, if that was even possible. That's when Sonny gave me a nudge, which almost sent me sailing across the room.

Bastard.

I flashed him the dirtiest look I could muster, then promptly took Vincent's hand, and shook it like a Polaroid picture. "Pleased to meet you." I grinned. "I'm, um... I'm not much of a hand kisser."

"Jesus, Clarissa!" Sonny said, reaching out to steady Vincent, who seemed perfectly fine to me. He was tall, not Sonny tall, but enough that I had to look up to make eye contact. He also looked pretty sturdy for someone so lean.

Why the hell was Sonny so tetchy about a little handshake? Maybe Vincent just wasn't used to people shaking his hand?

Or people at all?

"It's a pleasure to meet you," he said, extricating his hand from mine. "I'm Vincent."

"I got that."

I waited for a moment, expecting him to say his last name, you know, as a courtesy. But he didn't.

"So, it's just Vincent then?" I asked. "No last name?"

Sonny groaned and Vincent nodded.

"Just Vincent," he confirmed.

"Like Cher?" I asked. "Or Madonna? Oooh, or Beyoncé?"

"I suppose," Vincent replied, and motioned for us to sit in the overstuffed chairs while he returned to his throne.

Sonny rubbed his hands down his face and groaned again. "So much for not saying anything stupid," he grumbled as we took our seats.

"I didn't say anything stupid," I shot back. "I was double checking that I didn't have to call him *mister* something."

Vincent cleared his throat, commanding our attention. What a guy. All he had to do was cough, and you felt compelled to listen.

"So, I believe you've had quite the adventure, Ms. Hunt?" Vincent said. "Sonny tells me you recently survived not one, but two near-death experiences."

I scoffed. "There was nothing 'near' about either of those experiences, Mr. Vincent, I can assure you. I died. Twice."

"Firstly, it's just Vincent. No mister necessary. Remember, like…Beyoncé."

I smiled tightly.

"And secondly, while I'm sure you *believe* you died, we can't really be sure, can we?" Vincent asked, leaning back and steepling his fingers under his chin. "Especially after your unfortunate… What was it again? Oh yes, your hockey incident. You suffered significant head trauma. What makes you so certain you died?"

"You mean apart from waking up in a body bag?"

"Yes, well, that was rather unfortunate, but you wouldn't be the first person in history to be wrongly declared dead. Did you know in 19th century England, it happened so often undertakers took to installing bells at gravesites with ropes that went all the way down into the coffins? That way, if someone was buried alive, they could pull the rope and ring the bell, alerting passersby that they weren't, in fact, dead."

"And if this were 1828 and we were in London, I can see how that might be relevant," I said, leaning back in my own chair and mirroring Vincent's deliberate, ridiculously elegant movements. "But it's not."

He said nothing, simply watched me with interest and I felt compelled to further explain what had happened to me.

"Okay, what about, and I can hardly believe I'm saying this, what about the werewolf that ripped my throat out? Sonny tells me I got thrown out my third-story glass sliding doors. What about that?"

Vincent cocked his head. "It all sounds very feasible, doesn't it? Werewolves tearing your body apart and flinging you into the street."

"There is nothing feasible about anything that's happened this week." I blew out an exasperated breath. "What's with all the questions, anyway? And more importantly, why am I still here, getting the third degree from some guy who, for all I know, could be some kind of deranged serial killer? I don't need this crap."

Vincent smiled broadly, like I'd passed some sort of test, and he was proud of me or something, which only served to peeve me more.

"Looky here, Mr. Vincent, I don't know what you want from me or why your henchman thought it was a good idea that we should meet, but I don't need to justify anything to you, or anyone else, for that matter. I was dead. Now I'm not. I know dead, trust me."

"I see," Vincent said, cocking his head to the side. "And how exactly do you know dead? Care to elaborate?"

"Not particularly."

"But, I'm curious," he said, removing the cap from his Montblanc again and holding it over a fresh page in the notepad neatly placed in front of him. "Tell me why you are *so* certain you were dead."

I tilted my head and stared at him.

Vincent smiled. "Indulge me...please?"

"Fine," I said.

I heard Sonny groan, followed by an odd clucking noise. I glared at him, then took a steadying breath. "I'm sure because I've died before."

I eyeballed Vincent, searching for some kind of reaction to my "I've died before" revelation. I had to hand it to him, he was pretty good at remaining stoic and seemingly unphased in the face of what some might consider to be a startling revelation. Pretty good, but not perfect. I noted a slight, barely detectable, quirk of Vincent's brow. He was surprised, but he sure as heck didn't want to show it. Interesting, no?

Vincent nodded at me. "Please go on."

Surprised and curious. Very interesting

"Would it make any difference if I said I didn't want to go on?"

"What do you think?" he said with a tight smile.

"I think you'd just torture it out of me if I didn't volunteer the information myself."

"Then you already know the answer."

"Fine," I said. "I suffered from DCM."

"Isn't that a rap band?" Sonny asked.

"What? No, it's not a rap band. That's Run DMC, you

dimwit. DCM is short for dilated cardiomyopathy. My sister and I were both diagnosed with it just before our tenth birthday."

"Sister, you say?" Vincent said. This clearly piqued his interest even more than the revelation about my previous experiences with death. "I wasn't aware you have a sister."

"Had. Poppy was my twin, but she died when we were fourteen."

"My condolences," Sonny said, dropping his gaze.

"It's fine," I said. "It was a long time ago and I'm completely over it."

I so wasn't completely over it, but I wasn't about to admit that to either of these two clowns.

"Do you want to hear this story or not?"

Vincent nodded. "Certainly."

"I was always in and out of hospital, getting poked and prodded and tested and examined. I was getting treatment, having surgeries, trying new medications. It was exhausting and nothing worked." I sighed. "Sometimes, I felt like Poppy was the lucky one. Sometimes, I wished I was the one who had died."

Sonny looked at Vincent. Vincent looked at me. I looked away.

"Geez, that's dark," Sonny said.

"Yeah, well, that's how I felt. Anyway, after Poppy passed away, my condition deteriorated rapidly, too, and options were running out. My heart was failing, and it was getting harder and harder for the doctors to bring me back."

"Bring you back from where?" Sonny asked.

"From death. That's what happens with DCM. Your heart stops working, eventually. One time, it stopped for seven minutes—that's the first time I technically died. The second time, I was gone a full eleven minutes. They really, really thought I was a goner that time. But dear old Professor Chaney somehow saved the day."

"Professor Chaney, you say?" Vincent asked, scribbling in his notebook.

"Phillip Chaney. That's with one N and an E."

"He sounds like quite the miracle worker," Sonny said, glancing at Vincent.

"That's what my parents call him."

"So, what happened? I mean, you look pretty healthy," Sonny said with a cheeky wink that caused my heart to go pitter-patter.

"That's because I am," I replied.

That's when Vincent subtly gestured to my scar, and I instinctively raised my hand and rubbed the top of it gently.

"They found you a donor, didn't they?" he said, the barest hint of a frown creasing his brow.

"They did indeed," I replied, trying to shake the melancholy as it washed over me. You'd think I'd have been used to it. It had been over ten years, after all, and yet the overwhelming sadness of being an organ recipient still slugged me right in the guts every time I thought about it.

"And this makes you sad?" Vincent asked.

"Yes," I replied. "And no. I mean, no because I'm alive, right? I'm alive and well and living my best life."

"Sounds like a good outcome to me," Sonny said.

"It would be, if living hadn't come at someone else's expense."

I was greeted by two frowning faces.

"Do you know what it does to a person, knowing someone had to die, just so you could live?" I asked.

"I would imagine it would be quite…unsettling," Vincent said.

I snorted. "That's one way of putting it."

There was a long silence.

"Shall I continue?" I asked.

Vincent nodded. "Please do."

"Okay, so, they found a donor, and the next thing I know I'm being prepped for surgery," I gestured to my scar. "Eight hours later, I woke up in recovery with a brand-new ticker, and more energy than the bunny."

Vincent looked puzzled. "What bunny?"

"You know, with the batteries," I replied.

Vincent's expression didn't change.

"It's a character in an advertising campaign," Sonny explained. "Nothing you need to concern yourself with."

How could someone so attractive be so damn rude?

"So, your recovery went well, then?" Vincent continued, clearly bored with the bunny talk.

I chuckled. "Are you kidding me? From that point on, I was a walking, talking miracle." I paused. "A medical miracle, that is. Not a Godly one."

"Of course," Vincent replied with a nod.

"Within three weeks, I had recovered completely."

Vincent's brows shoot up. "Is that so?"

"I know, right? I was strong, running around like any other teenager—no, not like any other teenager," I corrected. "*Better*. I outran, outdanced, out-everythinged every single one of my friends and cousins; even Drew and he almost qualified for the Olympics once."

"That so?" Sonny said, seemingly impressed. "What event?"

"Um, synchronized swimming," I mumbled. "*Solo* synchronized swimming."

Sonny's lips quirked at the edges.

He had nice lips.

He had nice everything.

"Well, isn't that impressive," Vincent interjected. "You were saying?"

"What was I saying?"

"You were talking about your new heart," Sonny prompted.

"Right. Yes. The new heart suited me well."

Vincent and Sonny weren't the first people to be rendered speechless by the tale of my miraculous recovery. A parade of specialists had examined me over the years, pathologists, radiographers, cardiovascular surgeons, hematologists. All experts in their fields, and each of them utterly perplexed by just how impossibly perfect my recovery had been.

From the day I received my new heart, I'd never been sick. I know a lot of people say it. *Oh no, I don't need to worry about getting vaccinated. I never get sick,* and then spend two weeks in bed with the flu every winter. But when I say I've never been sick, I mean it literally. No colds, no flu, no COVID, no gastro. Not even so much as a hangover. I couldn't have been any healthier if I drank kale smoothies and did Bikram yoga for three hours a day which, PS, I did not.

Of course, that was until I got beaned with the hockey puck, attacked by a werewolf, and died all over again. Twice.

Sonny had gotten progressively pastier and sweatier as I shared my story. I leaned in and squinted at him. "Are you okay? You look like you've seen… You look unwell."

"When?" Sonny said.

"Um, now. You've gone all shiny—"

"No, when did you have your heart transplant?"

"Oh, um, ten years ago," I said. "When I was sixteen."

Sonny stood and stalked to the fully stocked liquor trolley in the corner of Vincent's office, spun around and walked back to me. I fought the urge to flinch.

"Are you sure?"

"Am I sure when I had my heart transplant? What kind of question—"

He glared at me and I could see the urgency in his eyes. "Yes, I'm sure. It'll be ten years, this May."

Sonny ran his hands through his hair. His biceps flexed, which made me tingle in the nicest way.

"Let's not get ahead of ourselves, Sonny," Vincent said. "It might not be what we think."

What the hell was he talking about? I did not like the sound of that. At all. Maybe it was time to make my exit.

"Look, as fun as this has been... Actually, it's been weird and disturbing and not really fun at all, but whatever. Anyway, I think it's time I left." I stood and glanced between Vincent and Sonny. Neither of them moved. They simply stared at me.

"Okay then. Well, I'm off, and don't take this wrong, but I hope I never run into either of you again. Nothing personal."

Vincent's face remained impassive as he watched me straighten. "Clarissa, please sit down." He gestured to the chair I'd just vacated.

"Thanks, but no." I turned to Sonny. "Are you going to show me out or do I have to find the way by myself?"

"Clarissa, please sit," Vincent repeated.

"I don't think so."

"Sit."

Sonny snort-coughed to stifle a not-so-subtle laugh that I was too livid to acknowledge.

"Sit?" I said. "Did you tell me to *SIT*? What am I, a *dog*? You don't speak to me like that. Nobody speaks to me like that. I will not sit. But I will leave." I turned toward the door, a little surprised that Sonny wasn't trying to stop me or making some kind of tasteless dog joke. I didn't miss the *I told you so* look he shot Vincent, though.

I hustled, as quickly as my aching, blistered feet allowed, straight for the office doors. As I reached for the knob, I felt a hand land on my shoulder, which of course made me spin around and shriek like a startled banshee.

Vincent had closed the fifteen meters that separated us without making so much as a peep. Or a whisper. Or a squeak. And he did it so quickly, I wasn't sure if he'd walked or flown.

"Clarissa," he said in a soothing tone that had an oddly calming effect on my fraying nerves.

"Stop saying my name like that," I said.

"Like what?"

"Like you're my friend. Like you know me."

"But I do know you."

"You know nothing about me."

"Really? I know about your love of the sparkly vampire."

Good God, was there anyone who didn't know about that?

"I know about your aversion to spiders and love of salted caramel ice cream. And I know about Azrael," he said, positioning himself so we were face-to-face (or more my face to his chest because, like I said, he was a tall unit).

I felt my eyes widen and my mouth pop open. "How—how do you know about Azrael?"

Vincent winked. "You'd be surprised by what I know about you, Clarissa."

"Ohmygod, are *you* the stalker?" I glared at Sonny over Vincent's shoulder. "Nice one, Einstein. Way to go and introduce me to this nut job. He's probably got a dark room filled with tele-photo pics of me. I bet you've even got a Buffy Bot, only it wouldn't be a Buffy Bot because it would be a *me*-shaped bot. You built a Clarissa Bot, didn't you, you perv?"

"What's your obsession with stalkers?" Sonny asked. "Seriously."

"It's the 21st century. A girl can never be too careful."

"I can assure you," Vincent said in his even tone and undefinable accent. "I'm not a stalker. I have no darkroom full of photos, and I definitely don't have a Buffy Bot, or a Clarissa Bot. I don't even know what a Buffy is."

"Who."

"What?"

"No, who. Buffy is a who, not a what."

"Okay, I don't know *who* Buffy is. Now, why don't you

come back and join us, and I'll tell you everything. I'm sure we have much to learn from each other."

"Sounds like you already know everything about me," I grumbled, and hesitated. I must have been off my rocker. Here I was, one hundred meters below the city I'd lived in all my life, in a subterranean cathedral, and the only people who knew where I was were complete strangers, one of whom broke into my house and fought off a pack of werewolves that obliterated half my house; and the other who was very likely a creeper with body parts in his freezer.

And I was just standing there, accepting it all, like a big, fat idiot.

I should have been paralyzed with fear or getting my keister the hell out of there.

And, yet...

"Come. Sit." Vincent motioned to my vacant chair.

"Good dog," Sonny muttered. I flashed him a dirty look, as did Vincent, wiping the smug smile off his face.

"Please," Vincent added.

Reluctantly, I followed him back to his desk and took my place next to Sonny. "When we get out of here, I'm going to kick you in the onions so hard," I said through gritted teeth, a fake smile plastered across my face. "You'll need to go to the dentist to have them removed."

"You'll have to catch me first," Sonny replied. Although I was starting to get the distinct impression that he wouldn't exactly be running to get away from me.

"Now," Vincent said. "Why don't we start with you telling me what Azrael told you?"

"How about no?"

"I beg your pardon?"

Seems Mr. Elegant wasn't used to people telling him no. Yeah, well, he'd never met me before. "How about you tell me who the hell you are, what you want from me, and then maybe—

just maybe—I'll tell you what Azrael said to me," I said, crossing my arms over my chest.

Vincent's laugh took me by surprise. Its lack of humor did not.

"You were right," he said, glancing at Sonny. "She is a feisty one."

"She's a pain in the ass."

"Perhaps."

"Hey!" I said. "I'm right here, you know."

"Indeed, you are," Vincent said. "Fine, I'll tell you who we are and why Sonny brought you to me, but in exchange you will tell me what information Azrael passed on to you. Deal?"

I contemplated his offer for a moment and decided I didn't have much to lose at this point.

"Deal," I said, extending my hand.

Vincent waggled his index finger at me. "There will be no more of that."

ELEVEN

"SO, LET ME GET THIS STRAIGHT. You..." I pointed at Vincent, "...and you," I pointed at Sonny, "work for a super-secret organization called the Patrons Of Order that, amongst other things, monitor and control the activities of supernatural creatures who live alongside humans and are constantly plotting to enslave, eliminate, or torture us in some way, shape, or form?"

"In its most basic terms, yes. That's correct," Vincent said flatly.

"*Riiiight*. You two aren't high, are you?" I asked.

"I wish," Sonny said, cradling his head in his hands.

"You and me, both," I said. "It might make this bat-shit crazy story even vaguely believable."

"Crazy? Really? Think about it, how else would you explain all the strange things that have been going on these past few days, Clarissa? Not to mention all the unexplained mysteries of the universe; all the senseless wars and violence, natural disasters, plague, pestilence," Vincent said. "The Bermuda Triangle, Area 52, the Great Pyramids of Giza...Justin Bieber. And let's not forget, seemingly average people who come back from the dead after suffering fatal head injuries?" He shot me a lopsided smile.

"Well, that could have been a misdiagnosis," I said, defensively. Why was my voice coming out all high and whiney? "I've been told that in the early 19th century—wait, did you say Justin Beiber?"

Vincent cocked his brow and smiled.

Well, will you look at that? Turns out Vincent wasn't quite as archaic as I thought he was.

"Fine, but you've got to admit, this all sounds, well…nuts!" I said.

"I can see how this might seem unbelievable, but I assure you, every word is true. This organization has existed for millennia, maintaining the delicate balance between the human and supernatural worlds."

"Why?" I asked.

"Why?"

"Yes, why?"

"Why do birds fly? Why do fish swim? Why does the wind blow?"

I tilted my head. "Really? That's what you're going with? Lame pseudo-philosophical drivel? Do I strike you as the type of person who's going to believe that horse shit?"

Sonny gaped at me while Vincent grinned.

"No, you absolutely do not," Vincent said, pausing and studying me like he was contemplating whether to tell me a secret or not. "Fine. This organization was established at a time when the fear of the supernatural was greater than the fear of anything else. All manner of ghosts and ghouls walked the earth back then, tormenting humans as they saw fit. People were terrified of possession or the prospect of being devoured or turned into a creature of the night. To them, these were fates worse than death."

"So? People believed in things that go bump in the night. Lots of people believe in things that aren't true. You know, like those diet freaks that'll try to convince you low-fat cheese tastes just as good as full fat. Bull dust."

"Oh, Clarissa...tsk, tsk," Vincent admonished. "So quick to dismiss something you know nothing of."

Why did he make me feel like I was a kid and he was my grandpa telling me off for kicking a puppy? (PS: I would never, EVER kick a puppy!)

"Okay, so, let's say I believe you," I said. "Let's say monsters and ghosts are real. Where do you guys come in?"

"The Patrons of Order restored the peace centuries ago, and now we keep the balance."

"No, I mean *you* specifically. And him." I pointed at Sonny. "Where do you fit in?"

"The Patrons of Order have holdings right across the globe," he said. "But because of the size of our operation and the sheer volume of work we undertake, we're broken up into four regional jurisdictions."

"And you oversee one of the regions?"

"I oversee all the regions. The Regional Overseers report to me, and Sonny is my second in command. He oversees the Peacekeeping detail."

"Ah, yes, you're a Peacekeeper," I said, remembering what the stinky werewolf had said. "So, you protect things...people, I guess."

He nodded. "And I eliminate things, if necessary."

"That doesn't sound very peaceful."

"To keep the peace, sometimes you have to kill, banish, vanquish." He shrugged. "No two days are the same."

"So, basically you're a Ghostbuster."

Now it was Vincent's turn to stifle a giggle. Sonny didn't look as amused, though.

"Clarissa," Vincent said. "Paranormal activity takes place all the time. It's a constant battle between good and evil, light and dark, the pure and the tainted. People are scared, they're confused." Vincent shrugged. "Who they gonna call?"

"Ha!" I threw my head back and laughed. "You know *Ghost-busters*. And here I thought you didn't have it in you." I held my palm up to Vincent. "High five."

He didn't move.

"Come on. Up high. Don't leave me hanging," I said. He didn't reply of course, so I high fived myself, and scowled at him.

"You judge quickly, don't you?" Vincent asked.

"Judge? *Me*? I don't judge. I'm not even remotely judgey. Okay, sometimes I can be a little judgey if stuff is, you know, lame. Like if someone wears socks with slides, or listens to Bon Jovi, or eats facon, or drinks cheap champagne, or someone who buys eveningwear off the rack. Who even does that?"

Vincent and Sonny both had a look, you know, like they didn't understand what I was saying, or rather, didn't believe what I was saying. "Okay, fine. I'm totally judgy. But did you have to go and be so judgy about my judginess? Who's being judgy now?"

I'd been standing there far too long, rambling like a fool, and while I still had so many questions related to my moral outrage over Vincent's ridiculous, yet seemingly astute, summation of my character, they'd have to wait.

"So, um, is this a free service you provide?" I asked, deliberately changing the subject. "Or do people pay you? I mean, how does it work? You save me from a demon, and I give you my first born?"

Vincent simply shook his head.

"Don't be ridiculous," Sonny scoffed. "We haven't performed a ritual human sacrifice for at least four or five hundred—"

Vincent shot Sonny the saltiest death stare I'd ever seen, and Sonny stiffened immediately.

"Never," Sonny corrected himself. "We haven't performed a ritual human sacrifice for four or five hundred *nevers*."

Nice save. Not.

Mental note: don't mention human sacrifices around Sonny or Vincent ever again. This is one piece of information I didn't want to know.

"We don't require any compensation for the work we do," Vincent said, redirecting the subject. "We have, let's call them backers."

"Like affiliates?" I asked, perking up at the thought. Affiliates were totally my jam. Sponsorships, endorsements, collaborations, the lot.

I might have been unwittingly thrust into this new world of werewolves and things that go bump in the night, but by day, I was still a badass Digital Content Manager.

My whole career revolved around sponsorships and collabs. Maybe I should ask who runs their social platforms. Seemed like it would be a really interesting gig, and clearly money would be no object.

Mental note: Google Patrons of Order and press Vincent for the deets about who handles their socials.

"Yes, I suppose you could say that. We are funded by a conglomerate of sympathizers."

"And who exactly are these sympathizers?"

"Well, without getting too specific, several monarchies, more than two dozen republic nations, oh, and the church."

"Which church?"

"All of them, actually."

"*All* of them?"

Vincent nodded. "Certainly. From Hindus to Scientologists, and everyone in between."

I chuckled, but when I realized I was the only one, I

coughed a little to hide my laughter. "So, let me get this straight, somehow you've managed to convince religions—organizations that haven't been able to see eye-to-eye on anything in the history of *ever*—that not only do monsters and goblins exist, but that they should *pay* you to protect them from them?"

Sonny slow-clapped and the urge to kick him got stronger. "I think she's got it," he said.

"This has to be a scam," I said, but they both shook their heads.

"Every religion has its own doctrines that deal with the paranormal world, Clarissa," Vincent said. "When you've seen the destruction a poltergeist can cause, or a vampire for that matter, you'd be surprised—"

"Wait, hold it," I said, raising my hands. "Are you telling me vampires are real? I mean, really real. That crack about Dracula before wasn't a joke?"

Sonny shook his head. "Nope. Not a joke."

"Of course, vampires are real." Vincent looked at Sonny and frowned. "She genuinely doesn't know any of this."

"Doesn't look like it."

"What else?" I asked, ignoring the fact that they were talking about me like I wasn't there, *again*.

"What else what?" Sonny asked.

And I was the dumb one.

"The beasties. The bitey, scratchy, creepy-crawly things. What else is real?"

"Well, obviously werewolves are real," Vincent said. "All types of shifters, really."

Obviously.

"Poltergeist, phantasms."

"And witches, warlocks, sorcerers," Sonny added.

Ooookaaaaay.

"Demons. There are hundreds of species of those. Then

you've got mermaids, Sirens, mermen, kraken," Vincent continued.

I blew out a quick, steadying breath.

"Zombies. Angels. Dragons. Gnomes. Faeries."

"Oh, come on, really? Faeries?" I scoffed. "As in Tinkerbell?"

"Errr, not exactly," Sonny said, with a smirk. "They're a little..." He paused, presumably searching for the right word.

"A little what?" I asked.

"Well, firstly, they're bigger than you'd think," he said.

"How much bigger?"

"In human form," Vincent said. "Big, like Sonny."

Sonny shifted his massive frame and I tried hard to imagine him as a six-foot-four faerie.

"In faerie form, they're closer to ten or fifteen feet tall."

"Oh, they are not," I scoffed.

"It's true," Sonny added. "And they have wicked, bad tempers, too."

"They're powerful, deadly, and quite frankly, most creatures that dwell in the Inner World are terrified of them."

"I need to sit down," I said, scrubbing a hand over my face and taking two shaky steps backward. Monsters. Demons. Giant, cranky faeries. I just couldn't believe it. "This is a lot to swallow," I said, bewildered. "Also, what's the Inner World?"

"Pardon?" Vincent replied.

"You said most creatures from the Inner World are scared of faeries. What exactly is the Inner World?"

"Well, the...what did you call them? The bitey, scratchy, creepy-crawly things dwell in the Inner World, a place deep inside where we are all free to be our true selves, no matter how light, or how dark, that might be."

Gulp.

"Most of the time, the faces people show each other are fake. That's the Outer World; smoke and mirrors, deception and lies."

Vincent nodded. "It's true. Paranormal creatures and humans show you what they want you to see. Things that show them as good people, kind people, God-fearing, law-abiding citizens of the world. In turn, we see what we want, what we've been conditioned to see—average, unexceptional, everyday people."

My skin was starting to crawl, and an unsettling knot was forming in my tummy. Something about what they were saying was ringing alarm bells.

"On the inside, however," Sonny continued. "Behind the mask, that's where you'll find someone's true face. A werewolf, a vampire, a demon, even a fairy can appear to be like you or me or any other human. But, behind the facade, they're anything but."

"That's the Inner World," I rasped.

Sonny tapped the side of his nose and pointed at me.

Strangely, it all was making a weird kind of sense. "It sounds exactly like the online world," I said.

"How's that?" Vincent asked.

"We'll, it's all smoke and mirrors, isn't it? Everyone posting about how perfectly amazing their lives are—perfect homes, perfect kids, perfect holidays, and perfect bodies. But it's all just a carefully curated farce."

"Because nobody's perfect?" Sonny asked.

"Exactly. On the outside, everything seems ideal, immaculately curated. Inside, well, I could name more than one influencer who spends their Friday nights watching *Grease* on Prime and crying into a tub of Ben and Jerry's."

"Seems our two worlds have more in common than I'd imagined," Vincent said.

I nodded. "Indeed."

I looked at Vincent through narrowed eyes. "So, what are you, then?" I asked.

"I'm human," he replied coolly.

I chuckled. "Why do I find that hard to believe?"

"No, it's true," Sonny said. "Vincent is very much human."

"But?" I said, making the universal hurry-up motion with my right hand.

"But what?" Vincent asked.

"There's a but coming, for sure. No way in heaven or hell, assuming either of them even exists, would these Patrons people put every day, average, Vinnie from the Block in charge of everything."

For the second time that night, Sonny seemingly choked on nothing.

"Firstly," Vincent snapped. "Never call me Vinnie from the Block again."

"Wow, someone doesn't have a sense of humor," I mumbled. "Cheekbones for days, but no humor."

"Secondly, of course heaven and hell exist. I thought you of all people would be a woman of faith, Clarissa."

"Why me?"

"And thirdly, you're right. I'm not average, but I promise, I am human."

I thought about the Warhol print. "Okay, I'll play. Tell me, how old are you?"

"Quite old," he replied.

"Can you give me a ballpark?"

"Why don't you guess?"

"Okay, I'm game. Are you Woodstock old?"

Vincent smiled and shook his head. "Older."

"Um, are you World War II old?"

He shook his head again.

"World War I?"

Sonny rolled his eyes. "We're going to be here all night, at this rate."

"You got somewhere you need to be?" I asked.

He looked at his watch. "As a matter of fact…"

A sudden rush of jealousy slammed into me which was unexpected, to say the least. I bet he was going to bump uglies with Rebecca. I bet she was all Mistress of Pain under that button-down facade. I bet she had a closet full of gag balls and riding crops. She might have everyone else fooled, but not me.

I turned back to Vincent. "Are you American Civil War old?"

"Oh, for pity's sake." Sonny plopped back down on the armchair. "Just put her out of her misery, Vincent, please. Some of us have a life."

I scowled at him. I had a life. I had a great life. Maybe I didn't go flouncing around playing with the Dungeon Mistress, but I still—

"Very well," Vincent conceded. "Let's just say the Battle of Hastings… I was there."

I gasped. "Really?"

Sonny tutted. "Do I need to explain the Battle of Hastings to you?"

"*I know about the Battle of Hastings*," I snapped, which probably wasn't entirely necessary. "We spent half a term on it in Mr. Crawford's year ten history class." I counted off on my fingers. "Normans vs. Saxons. King Harold. Big battle. Took place in… in…" I paused and locked eyes with Vincent. "1066."

He nodded.

"But that was 900 years ago."

"And even then, I was more than a couple of centuries old."

Wow. I had to get the number of his plastic surgeon.

"So, I'm meant to believe you're like a thousand years old?" I said, crossing my arms. "Seriously?"

"And then some," Sonny said, sulking in his chair.

"Well, you're either bat-shit crazy, which I'm leaning heavily toward, or you've had some amazing work done on your eye and forehead region," I said pointing to his face.

"I've never had plastic surgery," Vincent said, indignant.

"Please, don't treat me like an idiot."

Sonny snorted.

"You shut up," I said. "Oh, and the Warhol print?" I turned back to Vincent. "Nice touch. I mean, it really doesn't feel like a knockoff. It feels authentic," I said.

"Perhaps because it is?"

"And the photos, brilliant. Someone around here has mad Photoshop skills."

"I don't even know what a Photoshop is," Vincent said.

I threw my head back and laughed.

"What's so funny?" he asked, deadpan.

"Oh, sorry." I sobered. "I thought you were joking."

Vincent just stared at me.

"You weren't joking."

I turned back to Sonny, who was doing a good amount of chuckling himself. "Okay, what about you, then?" I asked. "What are you?"

Sonny stopped laughing. "You know what I am. I'm a Peacekeeper."

"No, that's what you *do*. I want to know what you *are*."

"No."

"No?"

"No." He looked pretty adamant.

I glanced at Vincent, who simply shrugged. "Don't look at me," he said. "Sonny keeps his private business very private."

"And how am I supposed to trust him when I don't know what he is?"

"He is trustworthy, Clarissa. That's all you need to know."

"I'm not convinced. How do I know he won't try to bite me or change me into whatever he is?"

I made a mental note to find out what type of monster Sonny was, and use the knowledge to extort favors, and possibly large quantities of ice cream.

I also made another mental note to get myself a notebook. I was making so many mental notes these days, I was barely keeping up. Better still, I could set something up digitally, like on an app, maybe.

Mental note: download an organization app.

"Believe me, if I wanted to kill you, I would have already," Sonny said. "As for *changing* you." He actually used air quotes when he said *changing*. "Even if I could, which I can't, what I am is a birthright, not some virus you catch. What makes you think I'd change you? You're whiny and spoiled and very disagreeable."

"You're such a tool," I said, eying him with displeasure. "I hate you. But I promise, I will find out what you are. Just wait and see."

"Over my dead body," he said.

"Even better." I smiled.

"Okay then, so I guess that leaves just one more question," I said, swallowing hard, my head swimming with all the new information. "What does any of this have to do with me?"

TWELVE

"WE'RE FAIRLY CERTAIN YOUR DONOR HEART CAME FROM A WEREWOLF," Vincent repeated, folding his hands neatly in his lap.

I blinked, frowned, then blinked some more. Had he actually said my heart came from a werewolf? Of course he hadn't, because that would be absurd.

A werewolf heart.

In my chest.

Pffft.

"Clarissa, did you hear me?" Vincent waved his hand in front of my face.

I met his gaze. "Yes."

"And did you understand me?"

I resisted the urge to slug him. "Yes."

"Then would you care to share what you're thinking?"

"What I'm thinking?" I blew out a steadying breath. "Well, firstly, I'm thinking you're both completely cray-cray," I raised my hand to the side of my head and traced small circles in the air with my index finger. "Like, coco-bananas. I mean, a were-wolf heart. Yeah, sure. Okay." I stood and circled my chair. "And I suppose the Botox injection I got last month was some kind of neurotoxin secreted by zombies? And the blood trans-fusions I've had over the years, they were from vampires, right?"

I snatched my bag and pashmina from the arm of the chair and stalked toward the door.

"Clarissa, this isn't a joke," Vincent said.

"Which is why I'm not laughing," I called over my shoulder.

Vincent appeared in front of me in the blink of an eye and I shrieked.

"You." I pointed right in his face. "Stop that." It was little wonder I was a nervous wreck with all his popping up in front of me like a damn Jack-in-the-Box.

"I'm serious, Clarissa," Vincent said, using that tone again.

"And so am I," I said, trying to keep my voice even and my hands steady. "Do you even hear yourself? You're trying to tell me I'm a werewolf!"

"I never said that. I said your donor heart—"

"*I know what you said,*" I snapped. "And, it's just ridiculous. A werewolf heart. Honestly."

"I know this is a lot to take in."

"It's not, actually, because it's just insane. How do you expect me to believe—I mean, how could this even happen?"

"We can't be sure—"

"Well, there's a shock," I said. "You know, for an organiza-tion that's supposed to be the authority on this kind of thing, you really know jack-shit."

Vincent bristled and I briefly entertained the thought that perhaps I'd pushed my luck a little too far with the jack-shit comment, and he might just banish me to the dungeon of doom. (Because I just knew the subterranean house of weirdness had to have a dungeon with rats, and moss growing on the walls, and absolutely no Wi-Fi or other necessities like...like mani-pedis or massages or UberEats.)

Judging by the rate at which the blood was draining from Sonny's face, I'm pretty sure he was thinking the same thing.

But Vincent didn't raise his voice. He just eyeballed me, without even so much as blinking. Which was a little off-putting.

I made my way back to the overstuffed chair that had clearly become *mine*, and sat. "Okay," I said, backpedaling. "Let's say I entertain this insane theory of yours, tell me, what makes you think it's a werewolf heart? Why not a vampire, or mermaid, or a...a leprechaun?

"Well, firstly, it's unlikely any viable tissue could be harvested from a vampire. They're already dead. So it's not that."

"Of course."

"Mermaids have this whole aversion to land thing going on, and leprechauns—"

"Don't tell me, let me guess, leprechauns have acid for blood? No, they're actually teeny green cyborgs? Aliens, maybe? Am I close?"

"Not even," Sonny chimed in. "It can't be a leprechaun heart because there's actually no such thing as leprechauns."

"Really?" I gaped.

"Really."

"Well, I'll be damned."

"Probably," Sonny said but I chose to ignore him.

Douche.

"What we do know, however," Vincent continued. "Is you seem to be developing some unique lycan traits."

"Like what? And while you're at it, what's a lycan? You keep saying it, but I have no idea—"

"Lycan is simply another term for werewolf. It comes from the Greek, lycanthropy; 'lykos', meaning wolf and 'anthropos', meaning—"

"I *do not* need a lesson in Hellenic linguistics," I huffed.

"Yes. Of course. Well, as I was saying, you are displaying quite a few lycanthropic characteristics." He counted off on his fingers, starting with his thumb. "Your inability to die—"

"If you want to get technical, I *can* die."

"Yes, but you can't stay dead, can you?" Sonny said.

"No."

I may have pouted.

"There's also the accelerated healing you're experiencing, the super strength, improved reflexes, physical speed...and if I'm not mistaken, you're probably also experiencing increased appetite.

"Yes, but in all fairness, that could just be because I'm getting my period. I mean, wow, I'm not even kidding, I eat everything that's not nailed down when—" I glanced up at Vincent and Sonny who had both blanched and were looking everywhere but at me. *Whoops*. "Um... never mind," I said.

"Anyway," Vincent continued without mentioning my period, thankfully. I really did need to learn not to just blurt out every little thought that popped into my head. Otherwise, I'd end up giving him all my PINs and passwords, and possibly the combination to the floor safe my father had installed in my wardrobe last year. Currently, it housed my passport, a family heirloom pendant thingamabob that my mum gave me for my 25th birthday, and every single miserable, humiliating, pimple-laden school photo I'd ever had taken. Some things should never see the light of day. School photos are at the top of that list. "While it's true that we know, how did you put it? Ah, yes, *jack-shit* about how it happened, we are fairly certain it's a lycan heart, and not at all human."

I was never going to live that jack-shit comment down, was I?

"But how is that even possible?" I said. "I mean, I can't imagine werewolves are proactive organ donors."

"Actually, they're not," Vincent said. "In fact, it's strictly forbidden for any paranormal creature to be an organ donor, for a number of reasons, including this one."

Vincent's eyes darted briefly to Sonny, who shifted in his seat, and then flicked back to me.

And what was that little look all about? It didn't take Benoit Blanc to figure out they knew more about my situation than they were letting on.

I made a mental note: pump Sonny for information.

Alternative mental note: just pump Sonny. Don't worry about the information.

"We're investigating, of course," Vincent said.

"Ohhhh, you're investigating. Well, that makes me feel *soooooo* much better," I threw my hands in the air. "Meanwhile, I'm getting attacked by monsters left, right and center. I'm dying so often I feel like I should just download the *Crawford Funerals* app instead of Uber, but it's all okay now because *you geniuses* are *INVESTIGATING!*"

At least they both had the decency to look sheepish.

"Unfortunately, what this means, however." Vincent had the good sense to ignore my little outburst. "Is that, until we find out exactly what's going on, we're going to have to keep an eye on you."

"What? Why?"

"Well, aside from not fully knowing how this happened, we also can't be certain how the werewolf heart will affect you."

"Affect me?"

Neither Vincent nor Sonny spoke.

"*Affect me?*"

"The biological makeup of the human body isn't exactly designed to withstand the extra stresses likely to manifest with the introduction of paranormal organs."

"You mean like rejection? Because I've been through that and —"

"Not rejection, but there is a strong possibility your body won't be able to tolerate the hormonal changes and increase in adrenaline pumping through you. You will likely experience marked personality changes—"

"What kind of changes?"

"Well, aggression for one. It's an inherent lycan trait, which could have quite an impact on your mental wellbeing."

"I did mention I'm getting my period, right?"

"Clarissa, please focus."

I rolled my eyes. "Fine. So, what else?"

"Improved sense of smell, acute hearing—"

"You know, I take back what I said earlier. For someone who claims to know very little about what's going on, you seem to know an awful lot about what's going on," I said.

"Pure speculation, of course," Vincent said, clearing his throat. "I assure you I'm as ignorant as you."

Hm. Now, why didn't I believe him?

I found myself feeling quite exhausted, and sank back into the armchair. "This can't be right. I've had this heart for ten years," I said, scrubbing my hands over my face. "Why is this happening now?"

"It's likely the lycan heart was dormant after the transplant; functioning just like a regular human heart. However, when you died, it reactivated—kicked into gear, so to speak—and brought you back to life."

"I don't understand. I mean, dead is dead, even for a were-wolf...isn't it?"

"No. Werewolves can't be killed in the same ways humans can. They regenerate at lightning speed, heal in the blink of an eye. A broken neck, massive blood loss, even disease...none of these can kill a werewolf."

"But you said I'm not a werewolf?"

"You're not, I don't think."

I glared at Vincent.

"But your heart *is*, and clearly it's having significant impact on your body."

I sat forward, and put my head between my knees. "This is a lot." I took several deep breaths that were meant to be calming (PS: they weren't), trying to stave off the tsunami-grade panic attack I had brewing.

Sonny filled a glass with clear liquid from one of Vincent's cut-glass decanters and handed it to me. I was hoping it was vodka. It was not.

"So what can, um, kill a werewolf?" I said between gulps of water. I should probably know, shouldn't I?"

"The usual; decapitation, incineration and, of course, pure silver through the heart," Sonny said.

Well didn't that conjure up some pretty mental pictures?

"So that's why I came back from the dead? Because I didn't die in a specific, and may I say, incredibly disturbing, way?"

"We think so, however—"

"Yeah, yeah. I know. You can't be sure. Wait, does this mean I'm going to turn into a werewolf next full moon?"

Vincent opened his mouth, but I raised my hand and halted him before he could utter a word. "I know, you don't know."

"No, I was going to say that werewolves don't just turn at the full moon."

"They can turn whenever they want," Sonny chimed in. "They also change when they're angry, scared…horny."

"I'm going to turn into a werewolf when I'm *horny*?"

Sonny shrugged. "Maybe."

"None of this is particularly reassuring."

"What can I say? You're an anomaly, Clarissa Hunt."

"Just what every girl wants to hear," I said, slumping back and sighing. It was clear I wasn't going anywhere in a hurry.

It was also clear neither Vincent nor Sonny were going to tell me what the hell was really going on, even though I knew that they knew more than they were saying. Of course, they didn't know that I knew that they knew more, but I did, and I intended to keep it that way.

Plus, it wasn't that much of a problem for me, anyway. While they might not be willing to tell me the truth, they weren't the only ones at my disposal who knew stuff. There was someone else I was sure could shed some light on the subject of my heart transplant: Nash.

And while he didn't actually perform my transplant, he did have access to the files written by the man who did, and that was as good a place for me to start as any.

Plus, you know, cute doctor.

THIRTEEN

I STARED INTO THE DARKNESS, willing myself to go to sleep, and cursing my paranoid—and frustratingly overactive—Imagination for not letting me. Although, it was probably unfair to chastise myself for being paranoid on this occasion, given I'd spent twenty-four hours in a secret underground cathedral with a thousand-year-old human, and a Sonny—whatever the hell he was—learning that every terrifying beast I'd ever imagined, every horror movie that had given me a jump-fright, every monster that had haunted my nightmares since I first saw the original *IT* when I was thirteen, was most likely lurking under my bed, or staring at me through the crack in my wardrobe door. They all really, truly existed…except for leprechauns, apparently, and not just in Stephen King's imagination.

Even faeries, which I had always imagined would be friendly and cheery creatures turned out to be Hagrid-sized, aggressive fluffers capable of ripping your throat out quicker than you could say, "Faith, trust, and a little bit of pixie dust".

And for someone who's seen *Peter Pan* over a hundred times, that was some truly disturbing imagery.

But that wasn't the worst part, neither was the revelation that the world was under constant threat from powerful, supernatural creatures. No, the worst part was that I was now part of it all. By dying, and coming back to life, I had unwittingly opened a door to the Inner World that I had no desire to ever step through.

Not that Vincent or Sonny had offered any suggestion as to how I'd come to have a werewolf heart beating in my chest.

That didn't mean they didn't know. It just meant they weren't willing to tell me. But given they'd kept their own existence secret from the human race for more than two-thousand years, the prospect of keeping the secret of how I came to be the proud owner of a secondhand werewolf heart, probably wasn't all that difficult for either of them.

It did make me wonder about the Patrons of Order, though. How *had* they been able to keep themselves a secret for so long? I mean, channel 9 couldn't keep the finale of *The Bachelorette* under wraps for more than thirty seconds, how in the hell had the Patrons managed to keep their own existence, and the existence of the entire paranormal world, out of the public eye and off the internet?

"People believe what they want to believe." Azrael's voice cut through the silence like a hot blade through butter, which made me shriek like Yma Sumac for the third time in a day. "Plus, you'd be surprised how quickly a problem can go away when you know some legitimate voodoo practitioners."

I squinted into the darkness until I could see the outline of Azrael's body. "Seriously, you need to learn to knock," I said, whipping my Magic 8 Ball at him and enjoying the satisfying *thunk* it made when it connected with his torso. "And stop reading my mind. It's annoying and rude."

"I'll stop when you stop hurling things at me. You know I bruise like a peach."

I sat up and flicked on the bedside lamp. Azrael was sitting in the plush occasional chair near the sliding door that lead out to my third-floor balcony, rubbing the center of his chest gingerly. "Your aim is getting wicked accurate, by the way," he said. "And you're becoming much stronger."

I smiled tightly and caught the Magic 8 Ball in one hand when he threw it back.

"So, I hear you met Vincent," Azrael said. "Still pompous and full of himself? He didn't make you kiss his hand, did he?"

I laughed, but it was forced, and I had a feeling Azrael knew it.

"He tried, but I refused."

"He wouldn't have liked that very much."

I shook my head. "Nope. He didn't."

We sat in an uncomfortable silence while I worked out how I was going to broach the conversation about Vincent and Sonny and the supernatural world with him. "Now would be a great time for you to read my mind," I said, but Azrael shrugged.

"You asked me to stop, so…"

"And you choose to listen to me?"

"You know what they say, be careful what you wish for."

Indeed.

"So, are you, you know, one of them?" I asked.

"A Patron? God, no."

"But you know who they are?"

"Well, yes." His voice became softer. "We move in similar circles."

"Why didn't you tell me about any of it?" I asked, pulling my knees up to my chest. "I thought you were, you know, my friend."

Azrael exhaled deeply and dropped his head into his hands. "You don't understand. When it comes to this kind of stuff, everyone, and I mean *everyone,* is strictly on a need-to-know basis. And you were classified as not needing to know."

"You still should have told me."

Azrael sighed. "You're probably right, but I really couldn't. They get real tetchy when their deep, dark secrets are revealed to human folk. Generally, if the secret gets out—" He ran his thumb left to right across his throat and made a gurgling sound.

While I appreciated Azrael's protective nature and good intentions, I still couldn't help feeling betrayed. "You could have given me a hint. At least it wouldn't have come as such a damn surprise. I mean, do you have any idea how much of a weeny I looked like when they told me there's a whole menagerie of beasties and scratchy things plotting to kill humans every second of every day? It was a lot to take in."

Azrael smirked. "I would have thought you might have had some clue, considering..." He pointed to himself. "Yours truly."

"I thought you were imaginary."

"Firstly, *you* didn't believe I was imaginary," Azrael said. "That's just something your stupid psychologist came up with."

"Well, I know that *now*," I said. "I just didn't know back *then*."

"Secondly, would you even have believed me if I'd told you about the POOs and the Inner World? I don't think so—"

"Hold it," I interrupted. "Did you say, POOs?"

"Yes."

"*POOS?*"

"Yes, **P**atrons of **O**rder. It's an acronym."

"And they know about this acronym?"

"Sure. They came up with it, so..."

I threw my head back and laughed.

POOs. No wonder they worked so hard to keep themselves a secret. I would too with that name.

I laughed so hard, and for so long, my cheeks and stomach muscles positively burned. And yet I couldn't stop laughing.

And laughing.

And before I knew it, tears were streaming down my face.

And I wasn't laughing anymore.

I was crying.

And crying.

In the blink of an eye, Azrael was at my side, taking his place on the bed as he had so many times before, and wrapping his massive wings around me.

"Why is this happening to me?" I slobbered, acutely aware of just how gross I was at that moment. "Haven't I been through enough? Haven't I had my share? When is it my turn to be boring and normal and average?"

Azrael snorted. "You? Average? Never going to happen. You've always been special."

I sighed heavily. "Believe me, I'm nothing special."

"Shut up," he whispered. "Everything about you is special." He pulled me in tight. "You're one of a kind."

I looked up at him and he cringed. "I'm sorry," he whispered. "That was insensitive of me."

"It's okay," I said. "I know what you meant."

Truth was, I wasn't one of a kind at all because, well, Poppy. Eight minutes older, which she never let me forget, Poppy was the first to speak. Apparently she said, *This is bullshit,* at the dinner table just as my father had finished serving up roast beef to Grandma, Grandpa, grandpa's brother, the chief political reporter from *The Age,* dad's lawyer Ziggy (he of the short-lived political aspirations, thanks to my sister)... Oh, and the Lord Mayor and her partner.

Poppy made quite the first impression, apparently.

She was also the first to walk; first to ride a bike and the first to learn to swim. She kissed a boy before I did and got detention for freeing all the frogs the year 12's were preparing to dissect in their advanced biology class.

She was also the first to be diagnosed with DCM, and she was the first to die.

We'd been two peas in a pod.

Until we weren't.

Which didn't make me one of a kind. It made me one of two of a kind.

"I've been around for a long time, kiddo. Even when Poppy was here, you were still one of a kind."

"You're just saying that to be nice." I sniffled, wiping my nose with the back of my hand.

"True," he said, and I laughed. I knew he was trying to help me forget all the crazy stuff I'd just learned, even if it was for just a moment, which I appreciated, no matter how unsuccessful he was.

"Of course, if you ever tell Vincent or Sonny, I'll deny it and fling you off a bridge for good measure."

"You know it wouldn't kill me, right?" I said.

"I know, but it'd sure hurt for a while."

FOURTEEN

I WAS SURPRISED Nash agreed to see me at such short notice, especially on a Saturday evening. I was, however, pretty disappointed when he suggested we meet at his office and not somewhere interesting like Gin Palace or Velvet Bar. I mean, it's not like I was expecting a ten-course supper at Vue De Monde or anything, but what did a girl have to do to get a drink around here?

It was eerily quiet when I arrived on the third floor of the Myer Clinic. There were no patients or personnel around, only empty suites where specialists and researchers worked by day— not the case at night, though. Seemed Nash was the only one there.

The elevator doors opened with a loud *ding*! that echoed down the dimly lit hallway. I stepped out and immediately cursed myself for insisting we meet ASAP.

Next time, we were meeting at a Starbucks.

At midday.

On a Tuesday.

I didn't bother knocking when I sidled up to Nash's outer office door, instead turning the knob and letting myself into the empty reception area. A single spear of brilliant light streamed out from under the inner office door, so I knocked, and entered after he invited me to come in.

Nash stood from his chair and rounded his desk, a broad smile on his face, hand outstretched. He was dressed casually, khaki slacks, charcoal Ralph Lauren polo, black loafers (sockless) and a matching Pierre Cardin belt. Understated. Stylish. Nice.

"Thanks for seeing me at such short notice," I said, taking his hand and marveling at how gentle his grip was. I mean, it was firm (nothing worse than a man with a limp-wristed handshake, IMHO); but it wasn't flaccid... or weak, because yuck. I thought about Sonny and how rough and calloused his hands were. (And big. His hands were so big.)

Where Sonny was brash and boorish, Nash was sleek and charming.

Where Sonny dressed like he was lead guitarist in a hard rock band, Nash gravitated toward tailor made, designer labels.

Where Sonny looked like a Viking you'd expect to find on the set of, well, *Vikings*, Nash looked like a polished, utterly perfect cardiothoracic surgeon.

Where Sonny made my heart race and body tingle in all the nicest places, Nash... Well, Nash also made my heart race and body tingle in all the nice places.

So, there was that.

Tingling and palpitations aside, these two men could not be more different if I'd specifically drawn them that way. Yet, they were like two sides of the same delicious coin.

"Well, I could hardly say no, could I?" Nash said. "You made it sound like it was a matter of life and death on the phone." He paused, giving me the once-over. "Looking at you now, though, I'm thinking it probably wasn't?"

"Oh, but it is," I said, taking a seat on the chair he gestured to. "Otherwise why would I ask to see you so urgently?"

Not for cocktails and tapas apparently.

"Because of my dazzling personality and rugged good looks?" He grinned.

"There's that, too," I said and felt my cheeks go pink. Nash's blue eyes sparkled with mischief and delight.

Oh, my.

"So, how can I help you? You really did sound panicked on the phone."

"Well, I was. I mean, I still am. I'm having some trouble with, you know, with the whole dying and coming-back thing."

Nash tilted his head like a curious puppy, and I had to fight the urge to pat him and call him a good boy. He was so damn cute with his floppy fringe and three-day-growth.

"We talked about this, Clarissa," he said. "You didn't die. It was—"

I lifted my hand in a silencing gesture. "Let's not go over all that again, please," I said. "We both know there's more to it than either of us is willing to admit, so why don't we just agree to disagree?"

He studied me for a moment, then nodded.

So, I nodded.

We'd both nodded.

Which was good, I guess.

Grabbing a notepad and pen from his desk, Nash settled himself on the chair opposite mine and leaned forward on his elbows.

"So, what is it, then?" he asked. "Are you sick?"

"God, I hope so, because if not, I'm pretty sure there isn't enough lithium in the world to fix this kind of crazy."

Was it better to be crazy or sane in this scenario? If I was sane, then I was some freaky experiment that was most likely the result of some poor werewolf dying and having their corpse desecrated. If I was crazy, then it meant I probably deserved to be in an asylum.

Neither option was good.

"I'm afraid I'm not following."

"Of course, you're not. How could you? I barely know what I'm talking about. I haven't been myself lately. Strange things are happening."

"Again, I'm not sure I understand. How about… Why don't you start at the beginning?"

I blew out a steadying breath. *Start at the beginning,* he'd said. Where was that exactly? Are we talking about when I died at the hockey game and came back to life in the elevator? Or when I was murdered by the manky werewolf in my kitchen? Or when I was kidnapped by Sonny and forced into the clutches of the Patrons of Order? (Okay, so kidnapped is probably an over-statement, but it's not like I had any clue what I was walking into.) Or was the beginning in fact ten years earlier, when someone transplanted a werewolf heart into my body?

"There's something wrong with me," I said, eventually. "More specifically, there's nothing wrong with me."

"Well that clears things up, thank you," Nash said.

"Okay, look, I died."

He raised his eyebrows.

"I'm not talking about the…" I tapped the side of my head.

"Not the hockey puck?"

"No."

"What then?"

Er, I hadn't thought this through, had I? I could hardly lead with the werewolf ripping my throat out scenario, could I? He'd have me locked up quicker than you could say bananas (because that's clearly what I was). I had to ease into that discussion.

"A balcony," I blurted.

"What balcony?"

"My balcony. I fell."

"Accidentally?"

"Well, of course, accidentally. I didn't jump, if that's what you're implying."

"I have to ask," he said.

"Yeah, well I didn't, so don't get all *RUOK? Day* on me."

He rolled his eyes. "Okay, so how *did* you fall?"

"I...er..."

Well, I was fighting a werewolf and, in the struggle, it ripped my throat out and flung me off my third-story balcony where I plummeted to yet another untimely death.

"I...um, well, I lost my balance, and..."

"How?"

"Oh, I was adjusting... There was a wobbly..." I stopped and collected my thoughts. "Look, we're getting off topic. The point is I fell off a balcony, and I died, again, and then I came back to life again...*again*."

"Clarissa, you really need to get over this obsession you have with dying. It's not healthy or rational." Nash sat back in his chair and rubbed the stubble on his chin. "Say, have you considered you might be suffering from TBI?"

"What the hell is—?"

"That hockey puck obviously caused an extremely traumatic brain injury that culminated in catastrophic injuries and the unfortunate body bag incident," he said.

Oh, if only it were that easy.

"It goes without saying you'd be experiencing PTSD or hallucinations—"

"I'm not crazy."

"No one said crazy," Nash said, raising his hands. "That's not a word we like to use. I was merely suggesting—"

"Well, don't suggest anything, okay? Just listen. There's something wrong with my heart."

He rose to his feet. "Okay, then. That's something I can help with." He took the stethoscope from his desk and draped it around his neck. "Are you experiencing chest pain? Shortness of breath? Palpitations?"

"No, everything's fine. My heart is fine."

"But you just said—"

"I know what I said, but that's not what I meant. My heart is fine. It's just...wrong."

"Wrong?"

"It's not... I don't think." I exhaled. "I don't think it's human."

Nash gaped at me.

This was going well, wasn't it?

"So, you suspect your heart is what, porcine? Bovine?"

"I don't even know what that means."

"Pig or cow."

"Eeew." I recoiled slightly. "No. Not at all."

"What then? Because if you don't think it's human and you don't think it's from an animal, what are you talking about? Something artificial? Mechanical? Because I can tell you, we're still a few years away from—"

"Supernatural," I blurted. "I think the heart that was transplanted into my body came from a supernatural creature."

There was a long silence while I gave Nash time to process what I'd just said and eventually, he cocked a brow. "I beg your pardon?"

"Supernatural. Specifically, a werewolf."

Nash pursed his lips; his plump, sexy, kissable lips, and frowned. "I'm sorry, but are you *crazy*?"

"I thought we didn't use that word," I said, aware that he'd closed his notebook, placed the stethoscope on the coffee table and was edging away from me.

"That was before you started talking about having werewolf bits in your body. This conversation," he gestured back and forth between us, "is completely nuts."

"Okay, firstly, that's not a nice thing to say. And secondly, I'm not nuts. It's true. I have it on good authority—"

"What authority?"

"Um, a leading authority," I replied.

"A leading authority on paranormal organ transplantation?" he said, brow rising.

"Yes?"

"And who exactly is this authority and what makes you believe—"

"I can't tell you."

"Why not?"

"For your safety. I can't risk you repeating any of this to anyone."

"Who the hell would even believe me?" he asked.

"I'm just saying, I can't have you telling anyone anything. They're kind of a cranky bunch."

"Who are?"

"The werewolves."

"The werewolves are the authority you were talking about?"

"God, no."

Nash rubbed his eyes. "If not them, then who is?"

"I can't tell you. You just have to trust me."

"I barely know you."

"It's a big ask, I know." Much to my horror, my eyes welled up, and I found myself picking at my fingernails. If mum was there, she'd have smacked my hand and sent me for a mani-pedi.

Because appearances were everything.

Nash remained silent for longer than I expected before sitting back down and steepling his fingers together. "So, let's say I believe you. Let's say something supernatural is going on here and somehow you ended up with a werewolf heart in your chest. What do you want from me?"

"What do you think? I want answers. I want to know how this happened to me."

"And what makes you think I have any answers? I didn't even participate in your surgery."

"That's true. But you have access to something I want," I said. "My file, and I want you to get it for me."

Nash snorted. "Yeah, okay. Good one."

"Really?" I said, excitedly.

"Of course not. Don't be ridiculous."

"I'm not kidding," I said.

"Neither am I. I'm not giving you access to your file."

"But it's *my* file. My personal, private file about me! I have the right to know more about my donor; specifically, their name, who they were, and how they died," I said.

"Um, no you don't. Legislation prevents health professionals from disclosing information that might publicly identify a donor or transplant recipient."

"But I *need* to know!"

"Oh, well then." Nash said, looking more uncomfortable than he did during the *let's sue everyone at the Royal Melbourne Hospital* conversation he had with my father. "If you *need* to know, then by all means, let's give you access. Let's forget about the laws and policies that ensure donor confidentiality, let's ignore the fact that I could lose my license to practice medicine, and that the clinic could be shut down. Shall I do that for you?"

"You don't have to act like such a dick," I grumbled.

"I'm not the one acting like a dick."

We sat in silence for what felt like an eternity.

"Okay, I might be acting like a dick, but Clarissa, this is ludicrous. What you're asking just isn't possible."

"Neither is coming back from the dead, yet here I am," I replied

"You can't seriously believe your heart came from a werewolf."

"I guess there's only one way to find out." I pointed at his computer. "Fire up that bad boy and bring up my file."

"No. That would be unethical."

"As would conducting an illegal organ transplant on a child."

"*Whoa*, there was nothing illegal about your transplant."

"Prove it," I replied. "Prove that everything was above board. You don't even have to show me the file. You check it. You make sure all the i's are dotted and the t's crossed, and if they are, I'll leave you be. You'll never see or hear from me again. But if something, even the tiniest thing doesn't add up, you have to agree to help me find out the truth."

Nash steepled his fingers again and gazed at me...for ages.

"Just pull up my damned file," I barked.

"You're not going to let up unless I do this, are you?" he asked.

I shook my head.

Nash sighed. "Fine, but if anyone finds out about this, it'll cost me everything. I'll never practice medicine again. I'd be lucky to get a job as a vet nurse."

I crossed my heart. "Cool your jets. I won't tell a soul. This'll be our little secret."

My heart wasn't the only thing I had crossed. My fingers were also woven tightly together behind my back. First confirmation that something untoward had taken place here, and I'd be spilling the beans to Vincent faster than you could say, "Wayne the wayward werewolf whipped a whippet with a white water bottle."

Nash glared at me and frowned. "Not. A. Word. To. Anyone. Remember that."

I nodded. "Who am I going to tell?"

"Well, that's strange," Nash said, squinting at his monitor and clicking the mouse on a few different tabs and buttons.

"What?" I asked, craning to see the screen from my shitty

vantage point across the desk from him. He might have agreed to look up my file, but he'd insisted I not stand next to him when he did it.

"You're not here."

"I'm not? Then, where am I?"

He glanced up at me and scowled. Even when he was pissed off, he was hot. "You know what I mean. You're not on file."

"*Aha*! See. I told you something was fishy. It's a cover-up."

"Settle down. I'm sure there's a logical explanation."

"Rubbish. A week ago, my file was there. Now, it's not. That's fishy."

"No, your file from a week ago is still here. It's your history that's missing."

"Okay, so *that's* fishy."

"Nothing's fishy. Geez, settle down already, I'm going to take a stab and say your file just hasn't been digitized yet."

"Oh," I said, drooping slightly.

"It's probably still in hard copy, though."

"And where would one be able to find this hard copy?" I asked, perking up again.

"Most likely in our record repository."

"And is said repository located on these premises?"

"Yes."

"Well? What are we waiting for? Hit me up," I said, leaping to my feet.

"I'm not taking you to the records room."

"Why not? Afraid of what you might find? Scared I'm right and there's some deep dark secret lurking in my file? A conspiracy maybe? Proof of illegal organ harvesting?"

"Are you trying to goad me?"

I shrugged. "Maybe. Is it working?"

"Kind of."

Nash studied me for a moment, then slowly shook his head. "Clarissa, just stop for a minute and listen to yourself. Werewolves. Conspiracies. Medical impropriety," he said, his tone softening. "Secret paranormal cover-ups. You sound as paranoid as your father."

Ouch!

"Well, when you put it like that." I flopped down on the plush, leather couch that dominated the left side of his office and covered my eyes with my arm.

Maybe I *was* going crazy. Maybe I *did* have some kind of acquired brain injury or trauma. When I really thought about it, how could any of this possibly be true? My life had been so normal, so blissfully ordinary before my run-in with the hockey puck. Maybe all this talk of werewolves and secret organizations really were just delusion fueled by an underlying subdural hematoma?

Much to my horror, I started to cry.

"Don't do that," Nash said, squatting beside me. "Please, don't cry."

"I can't help it," I wailed as a floodgate of tears opened and spilled down my face.

Oh, goody. I was ugly crying. Just what every girl wanted to do in front of the hunky doctor she's hoping will ask her to join him at Three Monkeys for a cheeky Cosmo and antipasto sometime. That'll win him over.

"I don't know what else to *doooooo*!" I howled. Werewolf pun *not* intended. "How else do you explain everything that's been happening to me?"

"It's definitely not normal, I'll give you that," Nash soothed. "But there must be a rational explanation that doesn't involve werewolves or other paranormal conspiracies."

He patted my arm in an awkward gesture that was strangely stilted for someone who relied on his bedside manner for a living.

"Let me help you," he said. "We'll admit you to the clinic. Do an MRI, run some tests—"

"*Noooooo!*" I wailed, even louder.

Oh, this was just getting better and better, wasn't it?

"No more tests. No more scans. I just can't face being prodded and poked anymore."

"Okay, okay," he placated. "We'll find another way. Maybe I can refer you to a colleague? I know a very well-respected psychologist who's been doing great work with…"

I glared at him.

"Or maybe not," he said. "Clarissa, you have to let me help you."

"Then check my file." I glanced up at him through my gloopy mascara.

Nash shook his head and sighed. "Fine. If it'll help you to realize just how craz—er, absurd this is, let's get this over and done with."

He stood and extended his hand to me. I stared at it.

"You're taking me to the records room now?" I asked.

He nodded. "Isn't that what you want?"

"Yes, but what about ruining your career?" I snuffled.

"Yeah, well, I changed my mind."

I took his hand and stood until we were face-to-face; well, face to chest in my case. He was taller than me. Not Sonny tall, not quite Vincent tall, but he had to be close to six foot.

The close proximity forced the breath from my lungs and all I could concentrate on was the amazing smell of his fresh, citrusy aftershave. Aqua Di Gio. Unmistakable and utterly intoxicating.

Nash cleared his throat, and I realized I'd been sniffing him. *Sniffing him! Oh God.*

I took a step backward, hit the edge of the couch and landed with a plop on my backside.

Yep. I was all class and elegance.

"Thank you for changing your mind," I said, trying to busy myself by searching through my handbag for a tissue. I found one, thankfully, and blotted at my eyes, removing as much of the gloopy mascara tragedy as possible.

Waterproof, my ass. Someone was getting a one-star review on the 'Zon come Monday.

He shrugged. "Seems I just can't stand to see you cry," he said with a gentle smile.

"Pushover."

"Trust me, I'm no pushover."

"Well, I'd say you are, if you cave every time a woman cries."

"I didn't say any woman, Clarissa. I said *you*."

FIFTEEN

THE RECORDS ROOM was located in the basement of the clinic, a quick trip via a freight elevator at the rear of the building.

When we reached a nondescript door at the end of a long passageway, Nash fished a set of keys from his pocket, slipped one into the lock, swung the door open, and flicked the light switches. Dozens of fluro lights buzzed and flickered to life above our heads and I thanked all the gods that I was able to remove most of the mascara gunk before we reached the basement, because we all know just how flattering fluorescent lighting can be on a pasty, post-ugly-cry face.

Shudder.

I would have had to kiss that imaginary invitation to Three Monkeys goodbye, for sure.

The room was filled, floor to ceiling, with filing cabinets and archive boxes, and what looked to be a lifetime's supply of empty condom wrappers strewn on pretty much every surface within arm's reach. Clearly this was the place staff came to do the ol' rumpy-pumpy between shifts or whatever.

It wasn't nearly as sexy as *Grey's Anatomy* would have had me believe. This wasn't a neat little on-call room. There were no bunks with rumpled sheets, no sexy scrubs flung haphazardly on the ground. Very disappointing.

"Now, don't touch anything," Nash said. He needn't have worried. Touching stuff when I knew this was the local shag shack was the last thing on my mind. I did briefly wonder, however, how many of the condom wrappers belonged to Nash and whom he'd used them with. I mean, a looker like him had to have the nurses and other doctors all in a flutter, all the time. No way this was his first trip down to the records room with a lady in tow. It was, however, probably the first time the trip would not culminate in a satisfying ending for both participants. Pity.

"Understand?" he said.

"What? Oh, sure. You don't have to tell me twice," I muttered.

"Don't look at any files. Don't open any boxes. Just follow me and let me do all the searching."

I stood straight, clicked my heels together and saluted him. "Yes, sir!"

"Don't be a smarty-pants. It's bad enough that you're even in here. If it gets out that I rummaged through patient files with you—"

"Yes, yes. I know. Relax. I'm not going to do anything to jeopardize your career." My fingers were crossed behind my back again. I'd do whatever the hell it took to get to the bottom of all this.

Nash pointed at me. "I'm not kidding."

"Fine. Do your thing. I won't touch anything." I shoved my hands into my coat pockets and nudged him with my elbow. "Go."

He nodded and made his way through the archival maze. I

noticed how familiar he was with the layout. Some of those condom wrappers were definitely his.

I followed close behind, covertly admiring his tight butt in those khakis and wondering if he worked out. Of course he worked out. You don't get glutes like that from eating Pringles and couch-surfing Netflix on weekends. If you did, my ass would be like Kylie Minogue's and not a bag of lumpy, old potatoes.

We reached a set of filing cabinets at the far end of the room where the lighting was much dimmer. Several of the fluorescent tubes had blown and those that were left cast eerie shadows on the walls and across the floor. There was one small mercy, at least. I'd look less like the chick from *The Ring* in the dim lighting.

Nash used the same set of keys he'd used to open the door to unlock the third cabinet in the last row. It clicked and he slid open the top drawer. I tried to peer over his shoulder as he flicked through the suspension files, but he was too tall and too broad for me to get even the slightest glimpse.

"I told you, no peeking," he said without looking up.

"Fine." I slumped back against the cabinet opposite and crossed my arms. As I looked around, an uneasy twistiness settled deep in my belly. I was beginning to feel claustrophobic. Sure, the records room was big, huge in fact, but with all the boxes and shelving piled high over my head, and no natural light, I felt like I was in that weird warehouse at the end of *Raiders of the Lost Ark*. Who knew what top-secret goodies were buried deep within the records room? The Dead Sea Scrolls. Harold Holt. Will Smith's sense of humor? JC himself could be in there, for all I knew. (If he was, I was going to sit him down and have a good long chat to him about resurrection.)

The uneasy feeling quickly morphed into an overwhelming and oppressive sense of doom—a crushing sense of foreboding, and my body started responding in a most unpleasant way. My chest contracted and blood thundered through my veins. There was a loud ringing in my ears that made me think I'd suddenly developed tinnitus; my palms were sweaty, and my mouth was drier than the Nullarbor.

Something was wrong; terribly, terribly wrong. I couldn't explain it, but I felt it in every follicle, every thrumming nerve in my body. My fingertips tingled and my jaw clenched so tight, I was pretty sure I was going to crack a veneer. It was like all my instincts were screaming, telling me the records room was no longer a safe place, and we had to get out of there, *pronto*.

I put my hand on Nash's shoulder. "Any luck?"

"Not in this drawer. Maybe there'll be something in the next one." He closed the top drawer and opened the second.

My anxiety was raging, and I was mega fidgety. "We should go."

Nash turned his head and shot me a puzzled look. "Are you kidding? First you practically beg me to find your file—"

"I wouldn't exactly call it begging."

"—and now you want to leave before we've even found it?"

"I've got a bad feeling," I said, shaking my hands in front of me like they were covered in excessive water, and shifting my weight from one foot to the other.

Nash straightened and draped his arm over the filing cabinet. "Really? A bad feeling? Are your Spidey senses tingling?"

"Mock all you like, but I've had a few of these lately and they're not usually a portent of fun things to come."

"So, this is a supernatural thing?" he asked. "Wait, are you going to wolf-out?"

"Wolf-out?"

"You know, fangs, hair, grrr..." Nash bared his teeth and growled at me.

Asshat.

"Well, no. I don't think so," I replied, although I wasn't sure. Truth be told I had no idea what would happen to me if I did indeed have a werewolf heart beating in my chest. Would I turn into a monster at the next full moon? Would I suddenly be allergic to silver? Eeeew, was I going to start peeing on everything to mark my territory? God, I hoped not. I couldn't even begin to explain that to my parents, and I'd never be allowed in the good lounge room again.

I pushed the *what if* questions out of my mind. I'd just have to add them to the other six billion I had for Sonny and Vincent.

"What about your file?"

"Never mind my file. I'll find another way. Can we just go?" I must have looked as terrified on the outside as I felt on the inside, because Nash closed the drawer and relocked the cabinet.

"Whatever you say."

The feeling that something wicked was looming had shaken me to my core and I couldn't get out of the records room and back into the freight elevator quick enough.

Of course, when the doors opened on the third floor again to reveal not one, but two enormous werewolves lumbering down the corridor, I just about fainted. The hulking beasts were ripping charts from the walls and flinging not-so-cheap artworks around like scraps of paper. They overturned everything in their paths, chairs, lamps, and, suddenly, I wished we'd stayed in the basement.

"What the fu—"

I yanked Nash back into the lift just as one of the lycans spotted us. Its eyes blazed crimson, and it ripped out a howl so loud that not only did it temporarily deafen me, but it also drew the instant attention of the second lycan. In a split second, they both dropped to all fours and charged at us, jaws snapping, and talons shredding the carpet tiles.

I pressed the button marked G on the panel to my right about a thousand times, praying for the doors to shut. They didn't, of course, and I thought fleetingly that this was the kind of shit that only happened in horror movies. What was next? Would we somehow become separated and one of us would turn up disemboweled or decapitated in a later scene? Would there be two creepy kids waiting for us when the lift doors eventually opened up on the ground floor, giving us the customary jump-scare—assuming we made it to the ground floor in one piece? Would there be a possessed doll? A treacherous storm? Maybe all the lights would go out? Wasn't there always a blackout or some kind of power failure?

The lights flickered overhead, and I froze, my breath catching in my throat. I really had to stop tempting fate with my overactive imagination.

With less than a second to spare, the elevator doors mercifully closed, leaving two infuriated werewolves howling at the top of their lungs on level three as we made the descent to the ground floor.

"Were they…they…werewolves?" Nash stammered. "Really werewolves?"

"Yes. They were. I don't like to say I told you so, but—"

"None of this is possible. Werewolves aren't real," he rambled.

"You want to tell them that?" I asked, pointing at the doors.

"That would be a no."

Thankfully, the elevator dinged, and the doors opened, signaling that we'd made it safely to the ground floor. Stepping out, we turned left toward the foyer and a hasty exit, when I spotted a third and fourth werewolf prowling the interior perimeter.

"Shit!" I said, grabbing Nash by the upper arm and pulling him out of the werewolves' sightline. "Is there another way out?"

Nash remained silent as he gaped at the beasts. He was pale and shaky and a little on the sweaty side. He was still pretty cute, though, all things considered, but kind of damp and he smelled of, well…tension. Not fear. Not panic. Just tension, like sulfur and perspiration.

"*Nash!*" I snapped my fingers in front of his terror-stricken face. "Don't freak out on me now."

He hadn't quite regained his senses, instead he just blinked at me. "They're…they're..." he repeated.

"Yes. Yes. They're werewolves. I know. What I don't know is if there is another way out of this building."

"They're..."

"Oh, for pity's sake, Steven. Focus!" Not knowing what else to do, I squared Nash up and slugged him. Pretty hard.

Nash spun around like a cartoon duck before I grabbed his shoulders and steadied him.

I could practically see the cartoon birds circling his head, and probably would have laughed if I wasn't afraid the werewolves would hear us.

"Is there another exit? Because, any second now, the two werewolves from the third floor are going to join these two on the ground floor, and it won't take them long to figure out we're here. So, how about you show me another way out, other than through lycanpalooza over there," I said, pointing toward the lobby. "So we don't end up someone's tasty snack."

Regaining his composure, Nash motioned to a small corridor to our right. "There's an emergency exit down there," he said. "It leads out through the back."

"Perfect. Let's go."

Nash grabbed my arm. "Nice right hook, by the way." He rubbed the bruise that was forming on his jaw.

"Sorry about that," I said.

"Don't mention it. Just remind me never to annoy you again."

"In that case, you might want to get a move on." I pulled him by the arm toward the corridor, just as the last elevator in the row *dinged*, signaling the arrival of our lycan buddies from the third floor.

We were dead out of time, so I picked up the pace and

hustled as fast as I could, tugging Nash along behind me. Lucky he was in shape and could keep up. Otherwise, one of us was going to be a werewolf snack—and the other was going to be me.

As we made our hasty exit, I mentally added a third item to my 'Reasons to Run' list:

1. To catch up with the ice cream van
2. Brad Pitt
3. Werewolves.

Legit list, if I do say so myself.

I could hear the lycans grizzling and growling from the lobby and knew it wouldn't take them long to work out how we'd escaped. A couple of loud howls echoed through the building, as I pushed open the emergency exit and shoved Nash through. Then, checking we weren't being followed, I quietly slipped out, and shut the door behind me.

The alley was poorly lit and smelled of rotten garbage, spray paint and, *eeew*, urine. Damn my heightened sense of smell. There were some things a girl just didn't want to sniff. On the upside, I didn't feel the need to mark my territory like a good doggo, so that was an encouraging sign.

I found a few pickets from a broken palette strewn nearby, jammed them under the exit door handle, and took off into the darkness. I knew the pickets wouldn't stop the lycans completely, or at all, but I hoped they might slow them down just enough for us to get away to the relative safety of the city streets.

"Nash!" I whisper-shouted, needing to find out where he was so we could both get hell out of there. "Steven."

Nothing. Not a peep.

Maybe he'd taken off and was going to get help? Maybe he'd taken off and wasn't getting help? Maybe he'd just decided to save his own butt and skedaddle? Maybe I should stop speculating about where the hell he was and get my own butt to safety?

I stalked through the alley, calling for Nash, but to no avail. Maybe he really had left me there. If so, that was a pretty shitty move on his part, especially since I was the one who saved him from being lycan *amuse-bouche*.

As I headed out of the alley toward Flinders Street, I heard something that made every hair on my body stand on end and the blood run cold in my veins.

I held my breath and counted.

One Mississippi.

Two Mississippi.

Three Mississippi.

The second growl was as low and menacing as the first, confirming that I was not alone in the alley.

"Nash, is that you?" I whisper-yelled a little louder this time. Of course it wasn't him. I knew that. His growl down in the basement was less than menacing and let's face it, he was probably already on a City Loop train, getting himself well away from this shit-show. Something I should have been doing much faster than I was.

It was so dark, I could barely see half a meter ahead, but I knew a werewolf was there because not only had I heard it, but I could smell it, too. That's one thing I'd learned about lycans so far: they stink...really bad. They were all wet fur, dried blood and oozy, icky pheromones that reeked worse than blue cheese and cabbage left out on a hot porch.

I heard scraping to my right and spun around, squinting into the darkness. Shadows, like great pools of ebony ink, oozed down the building walls and puddled onto the uneven pavement underfoot. It was in those shadows that I saw the glint of a silvery eye, and my heart hammered in response.

"Well, hello there. And who might you be?" I asked, as the werewolf emerged from the shadows, taking slow, lumbering steps toward me. It was enormous, much bigger than the ginger beast that had attacked me in my home. Even on all fours, it was over six feet tall and covered in coarse, black fur. On its back, a ridge of silver hairs stuck up like the spine of a stegosaurus.

I scurried into the middle of the alley where the lighting was better and there was a greater chance of somebody seeing me and possibly coming to my rescue. That's when I saw Nash's crumpled body slumped against the side of the building. He wasn't moving. He wasn't speaking. I couldn't tell if he was alive or dead.

The werewolf snarled and snapped at me, spraying glistening globules of drool the size of golf balls on the ground.

So, so gross.

I stepped back, not taking my eyes off the beast. Saving Nash would just have to wait, assuming he wasn't already dead.

"So, you're the human that can't be killed," the werewolf growled. "It's going to be my pleasure to put a stop to that."

"Don't count on it," I said, scouring some of the waste strewn around the alley for something, *anything*, I could use as a weapon. I spotted a broken broom handle and snatched it up.

"That won't do you any good," the werewolf said. "Wood can't harm lycans, you fool."

"Maybe not, but I'm betting if I jam this in your forehead, it'll still sting a bit."

If I didn't know better, I'd say the werewolf laughed at me.

"Wood is only effective on filthy vampires. And as you can see…" The werewolf stood up then, unfurling its gigantic body to full height which was, FYI, effing enormous. I mean, Shaq would have to look up, way up, to look this monster in the eye.

"Yeah, we'll see," I replied. "You'd be surprised how much damage I could do with this."

"Let's find out then, shall we?"

Without so much as the slightest warning, the werewolf with the silver spikes lunged at me; two tons of pure sinew, rock-hard bone, and snapping teeth, bearing down like a freight train. It slammed into me at full speed and I toppled to the ground, all the air forced from my lungs with an audible *whoosh.*

I wheezed and coughed and struggled to catch my breath.

The werewolf swatted at me and knocked the broom handle from my grip, sending it skittering along the cobblestones and into the shadows. It then turned and charged me again, but this time I managed to roll out of its way before it could take a chunk out of me with its razor-sharp teeth. It snapped and lunged again and again, coming at me without breaking its stride, but each time I managed to roll away until I, too, was completely in the shadows.

I realized then that the only chance I had of getting out of the alley alive, and reasonably intact, was by engaging in some dreaded hand-to-hand combat. Like I was Rocky or something.

Urgh.

As the werewolf circled me slowly, sizing me up, no doubt, I jumped to my feet and shored up my footing as best as I could. Drawing on my internal warrior princess, and following my gut instinct, I crouched, then leapt into the air with all my might, halting the beast with a well-timed, and let me say, extreeeemly fortuitous, side kick to the head.

The beast staggered backward, slipping on the cobblestones just enough for me to advance with a series of punches, and front and back kicks, that dazed the beast (and stunned me a little, too,) and sent it flying through the air, until it came down hard on the opposite side of the alley. The werewolf was groggy and disoriented but I knew it wouldn't take long to recover, so I gave myself a mental high-five for channeling my inner-Buffy and scrambled back into the shadows in search of my broom handle. I was a little surprised by how much of my Taekwondo training had come back to me, given the amount of time that had passed between that moment and my lessons, but at that moment, I wasn't complaining.

That's when I heard Nash groan a few feet to my right, and

almost wept with relief. I scrambled over to him. "Oh, thank God. Where are you hurt?"

He groaned and I could see he was gripping his stomach.

"Are you okay?"

"Not really," he wheezed, moving his hands and revealing a gaping wound that exposed deep claw marks that had ripped open his torso. There was blood; so much blood, and little fleshy bits everywhere. I was no doctor, but even I could see he'd been badly injured. Like, critically injured. Like, he needed medical attention. Quickly. Now.

I nodded, and reached into my back pocket for my phone, but before I could lay my hands on it, Nash's eyes widened, and his mouth opened and closed like a guppy.

I knew exactly what that look meant. I'd seen it before.

A gigantic paw swatted me from behind, its meat-hook claws tearing through my coat and ripping my back wide open. Hot, blinding pain ripped through my body and I could feel skin and muscle peel away from the bone. Blood, warm and sticky, oozed from the wounds, and my skin burned, but I still managed to scramble away before the werewolf swatted me again.

I collapsed onto the cold cobblestones. That was the moment I knew I was about to die…again, right there in the shitty little laneway behind the clinic that may or may not be dealing in the supernatural organ black market.

A shadow fell over me, blocking out the glimpses of the glimmering stars and moonlight that managed to peek between the tops of the city buildings. I looked up to see the werewolf, still standing on its hind legs, looming over me. Its silvery eyes positively glowed with anticipation and I knew it sensed victory. With teeth bared, the lycan descended and I silently prayed that it would kill me quickly and didn't just bat me around like a chew toy for shits and giggles.

I could smell its rancid breath and cringed as the long strands of drool that dangled from its mouth hovered over my face. The werewolf inched closer, sniffing me before its sandpaper-tongue flicked over my blood-drenched skin.

So gross.

"You're going to make a delicious snack," it growled.

"I wouldn't count on it," I said, just as I mustered what little energy I had, and thrust the sharp end of the broom handle I'd managed to grab between its third and fourth ribs.

I knew the stake wouldn't kill it, but I hoped it would stun the beast just long enough for me to scamper away.

The werewolf reared back, and howled bloody murder, so I scrambled as quickly as I could toward Flinders Street. I got within a few feet of my salvation before the werewolf caught up with me.

"That's it, no more playing. Tonight, you die."

That's when I caught sight of the dark figure emerging from the darkness. Who the hell was that? One of the other werewolves? An innocent bystander? I tried to call out, tried to get their attention, but the werewolf had wrapped its massive paw around my neck at that point and had started shaking me from side to side like a rag doll.

I clawed at the paw, barely moving any of the taloned fingers that gripped me. I felt the welcome release of eternal slumber beckon me, as my larynx buckled under the pressure of the lycan's grip.

Even as the sound of heavy footsteps echoed through the darkened alley, I knew it was too late. The werewolf reared back and lifted me up, by the neck, until I was hanging limply two or three feet in the air. It let out a deafening, guttural roar that might have scared me to death, if I wasn't already dying. Then it threw me to the ground and pounced on me, tearing at my body with its razor-sharp claws and teeth. The pain was, well, I can't even describe it. How do you put into words how it feels to be eaten alive?

My life was over and this time I wasn't sure I'd be able to

find my way back. With the distant sounds of the city fading around me, I tried to block out the sound of the lycan tearing at my flesh and crunching my bones.

I closed my eyes and thought of home.

Home, sweet home.

TO BE CONTINUED...

If you enjoyed Cross My Werewolf Heart and would like to read the second instalment in the trilogy, flip to the next page to read the blurb for Cross My Werewolf Heart: Hope Not to Die. All three books are out now, so you can head to your favorite retailer to keep reading.

Cross My Werewolf Heart: Hope Not to Die

"Have I ever mentioned how much I hate body bags?"
—Clarissa Hunt, Cross My Werewolf Heart: Hope Not to Die

•

I'm getting so sick and tired of dying.

I'm also getting pretty sick of all the werewolf mercenaries snapping at my heels and getting stared down by an uppity underworld receptionist who I'm pretty sure is a hell beast.

With my new ability to commune with the dead making me jumpier than a long-tailed cat in a roomful of rocking chairs, I'm pretty sure the end of my tether zoomed past me days ago.

At least the paranormal pains in my butt have stopped trashing my house.

With help (sort of) from my new band of not-so-merry sidekicks—Vincent, the immortal leader of the Patrons of Order, Poppy, the ghost of my dead twin sister, and Azrael, my imaginary childhood friend who, as it turns out, not so imaginary—I discover a diabolical plan to resurrect (pun intended) a forbidden experiment to create a master race of human-paranormal hybrids. A plan that was supposed to have been benched in the 1800s!

Still no closer to discovering how I ended up with a werewolf heart beating in my chest, I turned to my trusty friend, the internet, for answers.

Big mistake.

Not only did I not find out who was conducting the clandestine, inter-species transplant experiments, or how I got mixed up in the whole sordid affair in the first place, but I also unwittingly uncovered the red market: an online hub where paranormal body parts are bought and sold.

Nasty.

It doesn't help that my brain is all fuzzy with tingly thoughts about a certain smart-mouthed peacekeeper, and a dreamy cardio thoracic surgeon, both of whom are proving to be very distracting.

Perhaps meeting the werewolf and vampire elders at a super-secret meeting of the Patrons of Order would shed some more light on my dire situation?

I mean, it couldn't get any worse, could it?

•

Cross My Werewolf Heart: Hope Not to Die is the second book in the fast-paced, raucously funny and wildly unpredictable Cross My Werewolf Heart trilogy featuring sassy Digital Content Manager, Clarissa Hunt, and set in the fantastical world of #fangsfurandfreaks

Be warned, though, there's another juicy cliffhanger at the end of this book, and you simply won't be able to stop yourself from finding out the truth behind Clarissa's werewolf heart!

ACKNOWLEDGMENTS

You'd think this would be the easy part, right? The books are finished, the hard work is done (well, kind of) and now I get to thank all the wonderful people who somehow managed to put up with me talking about werewolves and secret societies for five years.

Like I said, easy, right?

Um, no.

Not easy.

Not even slightly, because every time I've tried to write these thanks, my pesky little inner voice has been screeching, "DON'T YOU DARE FORGET TO MENTION SOMEONE IMPORTANT, BECAUSE IF YOU DO, I WILL MAKE YOU FEEL THIS SMALL UNTIL THE END OF TIME!" (My inner voice is a neurotic Catholic, and it knows exactly how to inflict just the right amount of guilt and inner turmoil to drive me nuts, forever.)

But, I'm pulling up my big-girl pants, now, and giving it a go. Let's just hope I don't forget anyone.

Back in 2018, I attended a writing retreat, my first ever. It was five-days long, and during that time, our wonderful hosts and mentors, Lisa Ireland and Vanessa Carnevale (with a special guest appearance by the lovely, Sally Hepworth) listened, and workshopped, and encouraged, as I plotted out the novel I'd had percolating in the back of my mind for about six-months. I only had the title, Cross My Werewolf Heart, and the bare bones of a premise, but they were so supportive and so excited about my idea, that by the end of the week, I had the book (it was still only one book back then) completely plotted out on index cards... about 150 of them!

Of course, that original plot has evolved over time, but much of the work we did on that wonderful retreat still remains.

So, my first thanks go to Lisa, Vanessa and Sally, for setting me off on a writing journey that has turned into one of the happiest and most fulfilling experiences of my life.

I'd also like to thank Sherryl Clark, my Novel Writing lecturer at VU, who not only helped me find my unique voice - that special something that sets me apart from other writers - but also helped me to believe in that voice and nurture it. You built my confidence, taught me the fundamentals, and although it took over a decade to happen, set me on my way. To you, Sherryl, and to Tracy Rolfe, I say a massive thank you. You taught me well.

My heartfelt thanks also go to Lisa Walker from Inkabella Tattoo Studio (Wales) for the amazing artwork she created for my covers. Lisa took my visions for a little werewolf skeleton (I still love those fangy-fans!) and a great big gemstone heart and transformed them into a unique, bright, and bold reality. To say I love that artwork is a monumental understatement, and I thank you, for your patience and creative vision. One day, I will pay you a visit and you will tattoo that beautiful artwork on my body. That's a promise.

To my brilliant editor, Grace Bradley (USA), what would I have done without you? Your guidance, generosity of spirit, and patience, transformed the way I thought about my writing. You are wise beyond your years, and miles ahead of me, and I truly can't wait to work with you again. Plus, you corrected all my Australian English spelling, and changed it to US English spelling, which otherwise would have completely done my head in.

To Victoria Ellis from Cruel Ink Editing and Design (USA) for the beautiful job you did laying out my manuscript. Wow! I can't tell you how much I love the work you did, and how grateful I am for your kindness, patience and willingness to give so much of yourself to help me learn. I'd have been lost without you.

And, to Lee Taylor from Coffin Print Designs (England), what can I say? You took the beautiful artwork that Lisa created, and turned it into the most gorgeous, gloriously eye-catching covers I could have hoped for. Your work, your genuine desire to realise my vision, and your kind and generous nature gave me confidence. It'a been a real pleasure working with you.

When I took those first tentative steps, and committed to writing my novel, I was...I don't know how to describe it: reluctant, nervous, embarrassed, about telling my friends and colleagues about my dream. What if they thought me foolish? What if they thought I was living a pipe dream? What if they thought I was kidding myself?

I needn't have worried - not one bit - because I am truly blessed with the most amazingly supportive friends and colleagues anyone could ever dream of.

To Josephine, my lifelong friend, my sister from another mister, thank you. Thank you for reading endless versions of *Cross My Werewolf Heart* as I tried to iron out plot holes and clunky dialogue; thank you for brainstorming story ideas, and listening to me ramble on about paranormal creatures and plot twists ad nauseam; and thank you for giving me strength when I was filled with doubt. You've probably read my novel just as many times as I have, and you did it with love in your heart and a smile on your face. For all this, and so much more, I thank you.

To Sabrina, Eilis and Amanda, thank you sooooooo much! For beta reading a very long manuscript, for providing me with feed-back about my marketing ideas and merch concepts, and for your unwavering encouragement. You are astounding and I am so grateful to have each of you in my life, and forever in my heart.

To Greg, my favourite Senior Constable in the whole wide world, thank you for answering a million questions about police procedures, for critiquing my police officer dialogue, for hand-cuffing me and wrestling your wife to the ground in your kitchen…all in the name of research, or course! Thank you so much, YB.

To my beloved cheer squad, Andrew, Kylie, Arkin, Larissa, Raz, Clare, Ev, Angela, Magda, Jarrod, Mason, Tia, Cara, Tayla, Will, Zack, Isobel, Elissa, Donna, Melissa D, Mel H, Jason, Ben,

Sarah B, Pauline, Lisa W, Dr Jade, Emily, Jake, and Frankie...
what the hell would I do without you? I mean, seriously? I hope I
never have to find out!

And, to my writing tribe, Sue D, Jen, Sandra, Fiona, Charmaine,
Mel C, Ange, Sarma, Josie and Rita...you know what this means
to me, and you've been there with me every step of the way.
Thank you!

To my precious family, my mum, Paola, my Aunty Sandra and
my Aunty Liz...what can I say? You have always believed in
me. You have always made me feel like I could take on the
world. And, you've always encouraged me to follow my dreams.
You are the best of me, and I love you and thank you from the
bottom of my heart.

They say you should always leave the best til last, and that's
exactly what I've done. To my husband, my one true, my Rock
God, Steven. There really aren't many words that can express
just how much your love and support have meant to me.

It was you who told me to "write something you'd like to read",
it was you who encouraged me to learn, to improve my skills, to
go to conferences, to join writers' groups, to foster my writing
dream.

It's been you who has watched me spend endless hours writing,
rewriting, getting excited, showing frustration, loving my book,
hating my book, wanting to give up, but never letting me.

You are my everything. My partner in crime. You are what drives
me forward. You never hold me back. Everything I have done, I
have done because of you. Thank you, always.

ABOUT THE AUTHOR

Esther Del Zuanne is a mentor and communications specialist who love, love, loves to write lively, paranormal romantic comedies. Her heroines are bold and brash with boundless energy and tonnes of pizazz - and a dash of sass thrown in for good measure. Her heroes are daring, brave, super-sexy and oh, so, cheeky… Impossible to resist and easy to love.

Esther's debut *Cross My Werewolf Heart* trilogy, is the first in her **#fangsfurandfreaks** series, based on the misadventures of Clarissa Hunt and the mysterious Patrons of Order - keepers of the thin veneer that separates humanity from the seething supernatural world on its doorstep.

When she's not writing about things that go bump and growl in the night, Esther spends her time going to rock concerts, cruising **realestate.com** for beach-front properties she'll never afford, and watching her favourite horror movies over and over and over again.

She's been married to the Rock God since 1996 and lives in Melbourne, Australia, with two fur babies, waaaaay too many cushions (or so she's been told) and an embarrassing collection of Buffy the Vampire Slayer memorabilia.

Esther also loves hearing from readers and other writers. You can find all her contact details, social media links and sign up for her newsletter, by visiting **estherdelzuanne.com**

Milton Keynes UK
Ingram Content Group UK Ltd.
UKHW040648231023
431163UK00004B/84